WITHDRAWN

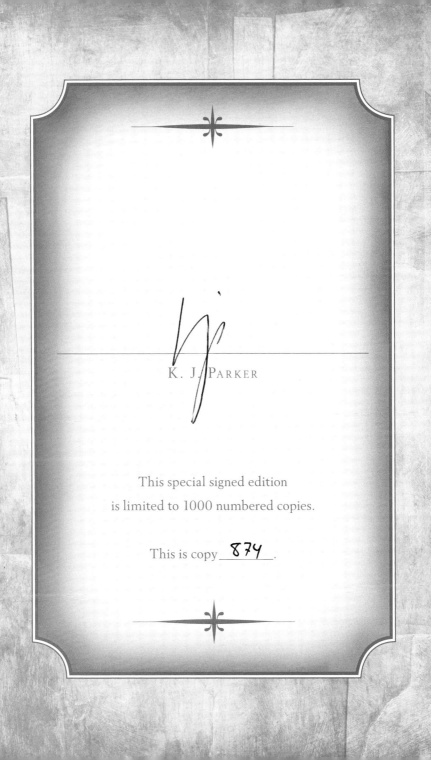

K. J. PARKER

This special signed edition
is limited to 1000 numbered copies.

This is copy ___874___.

THE LONG GAME

THE LONG GAME

K. J. PARKER

SUBTERRANEAN PRESS 2022

First Edition

ISBN
978-1-64524-060-0

Subterranean Press
PO Box 190106
Burton, MI 48519

subterraneanpress.com

Manufactured in the United States of America

Except...

THE BOOK WAS upside down. But she'd been reading it. I'd watched her turn the pages. She'd come in on the noon coach. Never seen her before in my life, obviously.

"What the hell," I hissed, "are you doing here?"

She gave me a blank stare. The book, I noticed, was *The Mirror of the Empty Soul*.

"Excuse me?" she said.

She was very beautiful. A tall young woman with straight black hair; elegant, severe white gown fastened at the shoulder with an old-fashioned grasshopper brooch; sitting on the verandah of the *Flawless Diamonds of Orthodoxy* reading a book. Apart from the book, her taste was clearly exquisite. I try not to lose my temper, but I don't always succeed.

"This is my patch." I was trying to keep my voice down. "If anybody gets assigned here, I'm notified. In advance. In writing. That's protocol."

7

"I have no idea what you're talking about."

People lie. It's unfortunate, but there it is. Depressingly often, people lie to me; and that's a mug's game. No human being is capable of deceiving me, because I can read minds as easily as you're reading this. So, if someone tells me something is true when I know it isn't, and I believe them, one of two things has happened. Either I've made a mistake and I was wrong (happens rather more often than I'd like, but not *that* often), or alternatively, someone's using *estuans intrinsecus*. Which is a real bitch of a Form, trust me. I can do it, but only because I practiced for hours and hours and had private coaching from the Precentor of the Studium. And *estuans* is self-defeating, because although it works (you use it and people believe anything you tell them), it leaves you drained and shaking, dripping with sweat and bleeding from the nose, which absolutely defeats the object of the exercise if whoever you're lying to is one of us and knows what to look out for. She, on the other hand, looked like she'd never sweated a drop in her whole life.

In which case I was wrong. But I could smell it on her a hundred yards away.

I GOT THIS posting because of a stupid mistake; mine. I bet some brash, stupid young lout in the diocesan supervision office that I could do his job better than he could, for a whole month. And I did. In fact, I did it so well that Father Prior transferred me from my beautiful prebendary stall and research fellowship to operational field duties. A man like me, he said, with my talents, stuck behind a desk; it was a horrible, abominable waste.

That was six years ago and the brash, stupid young lout is now junior precentor at Lonjamen, and I'm stuck here, eating rye porridge and leathery bacon with the hair still on, in shitholes like the *Flawless Diamonds*. My arse spends more time in a saddle than on a library stool, and my breath stinks, as does the rest of me. Trouble is, I keep pulling off these spectacular coups of fieldwork, and every time I cover myself in glory, I practically guarantee myself another six months on the road. The horrible fact is, I'm good at this job and I can't help being good at what I'm good at, if you follow me. I'm a better than average scholar and a tolerable lecturer, but when it comes to fieldwork I'm hotter than Army mustard. There's a lot of people who reckon they're my worst enemy, but you know the saying. If something's worth doing, do it yourself.

"Name," I snapped.

She rested the book in her lap, finger between the pages to mark the place. "Are you some sort of official or something?"

"I'm a duly authorised officer of the Studium," I said. "and I asked you your name."

She gave me a blank look. "The Studium," she said. "Isn't that some sort of school?"

Yes, all right. But I've never known it not work, except for this time. "I'm an ordained cleric," I said. "Which means I'm an officer of the ecclesiastical court, which gives me jurisdiction in matters of ecclesiastical law, including blasphemy and witchcraft. Name."

She shook her head. "No it doesn't," she said. "Not unless you're a what's-it-called, canon jury-something. Juridical. Are you one of those?"

"Yes."

"Have you got a badge or something?"

"We don't have badges."

She looked at me as though she'd just bought me and already my seams were starting to split. "I don't believe you," she said. "Go away."

Actually, for the record, I'm genuinely an honorary canon juridical, *ex officio*, on account of having been a serjeant-at-arms in the Reserve in my third year at the Studium. If you were in the Reserve you were let off PE and organised sports, and I despise being out of breath. But I don't tell lies if I can help it. And we don't carry badges. We don't *need* to. "Your last chance," I said. "Name."

"If you don't go away I'll call the landlord and have you thrown out."

Which, *very* loosely construed, constitutes an act or threat of violence against the person, which entitles me to use reasonable and proportionate measures in my defence. I grinned. *Loquar menti*; piece of cake. Any second-year can do it, and only a tactical-grade can defend against it.

Her defence knocked me off my feet, literally. I ended up on the floor, on my backside, with my head spinning. I gawped at her. Nobody does that to me.

She sighed. "Oh, all right," she said. "I'm Amalasomtha. Who the hell are you?"

FACT; WOMEN CAN'T be adepts. They're physically incapable of harbouring the Knack, just as men can't give birth to babies.

Except (there's always an Except); that's not actually true. A tiny, tiny proportion of women have the Knack. And, guess what, as soon as they're detected they're snapped up by Doctrine and trained as spooks, to keep a baleful eye on the rest of us—because, of course, no male adept would ever suspect a woman of being an orthodoxy enforcement officer. And, of course, we all know about it, and assume that any female adept we run across is a predator, after our collars. Hence my violent and uncharacteristic outburst when I smelt her at the inn.

She was an adept all right; I had the bruises on my mind and my backside to prove it. Also, the smack across the soul she'd given me hadn't been the purely reflexive act of an undiagnosed natural. She'd known precisely what she was doing, and she'd done it very, very well. Better than I could, that's for sure, and as previously noted, I'm good at this stuff. Credit where it's due, and all that sort of thing.

I hate mysteries. Something of a drawback for a professional investigator. Still, as I think I may have intimated, I'm not here through choice.

"Never mind who I am," I said, wiping blood from the corner of my mouth—except there wasn't any blood, needless to say, but it always feels like there should be. "Who are you?"

"I just told you."

There was nobody around to overhear. But, to be on the safe side, I'd used *aes grave*, so we were practically invisible to any but our own kind. Of which, I was prepared to bet my collar and all three painfully-won buttons, she was one. But if so, why in God's name not admit it? You can't slap a fellow-adept till his head spins and then pretend nothing's happened, that's just silly.

Sometimes I'm so stupid I wonder how I remember to breathe.

"Good book?"

"What?"

"That book you're reading. Any good?"

She frowned, then decided to answer the question. "Yes," she said. "Why?"

"You don't think it's carelessly researched, poorly constructed, wildly speculative and atrociously badly written?"

"No."

I shrugged. I wrote it, ten years ago. "Ah well," I said. "It wouldn't do if we all thought the same. You're Idalian."

(WHICH WAS, OF course, impossible. Except—

Idalia, if it exists, which is not universally accepted, is eight thousand miles away. Liutprand of Gallen claimed to have reached it five hundred years ago, on his way to the Moon. Edinhard the Stammerer wrote a detailed account of his wanderings there, riddled with internal inconsistencies apart from the bits he copied out of Gainas' *Travels in Permia* (Permia's about as far from Idalia as you can get, but nobody knows anything about Permia, either) According to Theuderic of Bingen, Idalians are seven feet tall and have their heads in the middle of their chests; also, he'd have you believe, when they read a book they start at the bottom right of the page and read up to the top left, and they write upside down. He'd have no way of knowing that, of course, since according to Litomer the Deacon, Idalian writing is a series of little pictures, not proper words, so no Westerner would have a clue which way up they're supposed to be, always assuming that the concept *upside down* has any relevance in this context. Oh, and—more far-fetched still—Aimeric de Peguilhan in his *Catalogue of Earthly Wonders* reckons that in Idalia, there are as many female adepts as male, and Idalian women give birth through their ears.

People say a lot of weird stuff. And just because it's in a book, it ain't necessarily so.)

SHE LOOKED AT me, with something approaching respect. Actually, I'm exaggerating. It was as though she'd trodden in a cowpat and found a farthing embedded in it.

"Keep your voice down," she said.

"You're Idalian."

"I didn't say that."

People can't lie to me, because I can look into any human head and see for myself. Blue for the truth, red for a lie, it's that simple. Inside her mind was a sort of soothing beige. She was all pastel colours, all the damn time. "You read upside down."

"No."

Well, no, not from her perspective; we're the ones who do that. So, no lie. Still beige. For crying out loud; *why?* So I thought to myself; this isn't my problem. An improbable person from a far country of which we know little has landed up on my patch, but if she's Idalian she's unlikely to be a Doctrine snoop, and since I'm not a political grade, she's not my problem, therefore can't be my fault. Possibly I ought to report her to somebody, but if I do nobody will believe me, and if I'd happened to come by an hour later, I'd never have known she was here. Nobody can prove I didn't come by an hour later; therefore, no action required. There, you see? Off the hook.

I wish my mind worked like that.

"All right," I said. "Answer me one question."

"Depends what it is."

"Answer me one question," I said, "and I'll go away and pretend I never saw you."

She thought about it for three seconds. "Shoot," she said.

AND WHAT, YOU should really be asking yourself (but you haven't, because I've deliberately distracted you with my meretricious narrative tricks) was someone like me doing in Sabades Amar in the first place?

I could fob you off with what I eventually wrote in my official report (a tissue of lies, naturally). I was at the *Flawless Diamonds* at that particular moment because I'd got off the southbound mailcoach and was hanging around waiting for my connection to Drutz. Which is true. But the southbound coach I'd been on had got in the evening before last, and that day's morning coach to Drutz had already been and gone. Not the same thing at all. See? I can tell the truth and lie at the same time. Bet you wish you could do that.

Motto of the field division since time out of mind; *we get all the rotten jobs.* And we do, we do. But some jobs are more rotten than others, and one man's rotten job is another man's self-indulgent pleasure. In my case, a chance to catch up with an old friend—

Wash my mouth out with lye and water. Except—

People make friends in unlikely places. And in some places, they're more likely to make unlikely friends than likely ones. The classic example of that is the House. Ask any senator; which side are your true friends on—not the ones you vote with and agree with on points of ideology;

the ones you meet for a drink and a good moan afterwards? And they'll all tell you, the other side, naturally. The guys on your side are the ones who'll let you down or stitch you up at the drop of a hat. With the enemy you can be yourself, because they aren't after that junior secretaryship or scared stiff you're a spy for the whip's office. Sort of the same in my line of work. Some of my closest colleagues would cheerfully cut my throat with a broken teabowl if it meant getting a junior fellowship with tenure. And, by the same token, some of my truest friends are the Enemy.

No, really. I mean it.

Take the particular example I was hanging round the *Diamonds* looking out for. He's—sorry, it's, but I always think of it as a he—it's a fairly innocuous specimen, generally doesn't do any lasting harm to its hosts, or victims if you really insist. It pops in, usually when they're asleep, burrows down into the dark, warm places in their minds, makes a cosy little nest for itself and hibernates, quiet and peaceful, hardly eats anything, you really wouldn't know it was there. I get the impression that its superiors aren't wildly impressed; a serial under-achiever is one of their more polite assessments, so I gather. But (it argues) so what? If it started making a nuisance of itself, throwing its weight about, screaming fits and bouts of gory self-harm, it'd quickly be spotted by someone like me and be thrown out on its ear quick-sharp, and how would that advance the Dark Cause, precisely? Instead, it argues, it's deeply and securely ensconced, out of sight and mind of the other side (that would be me), ready and waiting just in case some circumstance arises in which its presence might just conceivably be useful… They can't argue with that, it tells me, because they're so used to being found out, chucked out, sooner or later losing every fight they pick that it's hard for them to criticise one of their own simply for being useless. Which raises the question of why they bother; but that's high doctrine, and if I explained you wouldn't be able to follow it, trust me. I don't understand it, that's for sure, but that doesn't stop me explaining it twice a year to graduate students.

So there I was in Sabades, hanging round the coaching inn sniffing the passengers in hopes of meeting my old friend/enemy, who I had reason to believe would be passing through, embedded in the mind of a corn chandler from Obergallen who'd been reported by his family for acting a bit oddly in a very distinctive and characteristic way… Not that I had the slightest intention of evicting my old pal; but we have an understanding. I threaten to drive him out, though he doesn't believe me for a moment. In return for being allowed to stay, he gives me certain snippets of information about the activities of his colleagues (which may or may not be true, naturally). It's a little game we play, and it gives us a chance to chat and whine about our respective superiors, and that's absolutely fine. And I realise I've been calling it him, but so what? Go back and change the pronouns for yourself, if they offend you.

"IS IT TRUE," I asked her, "that Idalian men have four testicles?"

She blushed. "I wouldn't know," she said.

"That wasn't the question, just me being nosy. Why are you here?"

She sighed. "If I tell you, will you go away?"

"Yes."

"Fine." She looked away, took a deep breath, then looked back at me. "I'm a [some Idalian word] of the [several more Idalian words] and I've been sent here to do a very important job that I'm not allowed to talk about. And obviously you're a—" She hesitated. I nodded. "Right, that's fine. Actually I'm surprised. Back home, they tell us there aren't any, in the West."

I found that mildly offensive. "Is that right?"

"Yes. But we don't actually know very much about you."

"So it seems."

"When I was a little girl, my grandmother told me that in the West, people only have one leg, with an enormous foot they hop around on very fast, and when the sun gets too hot they lie on their backs and use it as a sunshade."

I nodded. "There's an element of truth in that. A very, very small one. We do have feet."

"I noticed. But really and truly, I'm not supposed to talk to anyone about why I'm here. And you did promise you'd go away."

So what, I thought. I've met an Idalian. And nobody can prove it. A bit like seeing a purple kingfisher—they're supposed to be extinct, but they don't know that. Unusual, certainly, but not significant, doesn't mean anything. Nothing I'm obliged to do anything about. And I did promise.

"Fine," I said, discreetly teasing a single hair from the back of my head. "I'll let you get on, then. Nice to have met you, and welcome to the Ozidan peninsula." And then I got up and walked away, without looking back.

I MET MY pal an hour or so later, when the City coach pulled in. I caught a glimpse of him in the corn chandler's eyes, before he had a chance to scuttle away and hide. I went in after him. You again, he said.

Me again. Actually, someone once did the arithmetic— I think it was the same scholarly clown who calculated how many angels can dance on the head of a pin—and came up with a figure of 203,686. That's how many of them— demons, he called them, but I don't like that word—are on active service in the world at any one time. Sounds a lot, I know; but think about it. In the Empire alone (and that's only a third of the known world) there must be, what, eleven, maybe twelve *million* people, so that's just one of them for every fifty-eight of us. And the other side are like us; they get assigned their territories, just like we do, and they're answerable to their area supervisors and regional, provincial and divisional officers, just like we are, and— well, there you go. I know them all, by sight and by smell, and boy, do they know me. So. Me again.

We did the usual, in the fraction of a second it takes us to have a long, leisurely chat inside some poor bastard's head. Sit down, he says, have a drink. No thanks, I'm on duty (because he may be a friend, but, well, he's on duty too. No food or drink. You don't know where or what it's been. You don't know *who* it's been.) It's all subjective, of course, inside a stranger's head. I see it one way, someone else would see (and feel, and smell) something completely different. I always see a marble floor, tapestries with hunting scenes on the wall, oil lamps backed with curved mirrors to amplify and project the light, my friend as a jovial fat man reclining on a couch, while behind us a log fire roars in a grate. So, obviously subjective. Smoke billowing out of someone's ears would be bound to be noticed.

I ask him for the information. He gives me the answer his superiors have told him to give me. It's a lie, obviously. I thank him. The fact that I get a lie tells me all I need to know. He knows that, and so presumably do his bosses. After all, we all have to work together all the time, so why make life impossibly difficult for each other? We know the score, and our side always wins eventually, and they accept that with a certain degree of, well, grace. No choice in the matter.

Then, business concluded, we can talk. He tells me about his impossibly demanding and unreasonable line managers. I bitch about the preferment committee and the fact that men I taught when they were novices are now ordering me about, telling me what I can and can't do. In doing so I let slip a few snippets (personnel changes; new directions in policy) that might prove useful to an enemy. He snaps them up without any indication that he's caught me out in an indiscretion. The snippets are lies, of course. Professional courtesy.

Then it's time to go. I've been inside the corn-chandler's head for two seconds. Three, and you start popping blood vessels. Till next time, I say to my friend. He grins; why's it always you, he says. He doesn't mean anything by it. I stand up to leave.

I think you ought to know, he says. And stops dead.

THERE ARE SEVEN inns in Sabades, and the *Flawless Diamonds of Orthodoxy* is far and away the best. So I slept in a hayloft over a livery stable in Long Alley, and woke up with a crick in my neck.

Why do we always win?

If you were my third-year revision class, you'd get a rather different answer, but since you aren't, here we go. We're stronger. That's it.

Strength is, of course, a relative term. Give you an example. An arm-wrestling match between a farmer and a locust could only end one way, but when locusts and farmers dispute the possession of a field of grain, it's the locusts who tend to win. They're weaker, but there's ever so many more of them. Sort of the same with us and the Enemy. If one of Them gets inside your head, it's infinitely stronger than you are. It takes over your bones, sinews, muscles, veins, nerves; unlike you it doesn't depend on any of them for its survival, so if it tells you to smash your head against a wall—no skin off its nose, but yours is a catastrophe of blood and splinters. Its duty is to mess you up as badly as it possibly can, short of killing you; except— If it can use you to further the long-term aims of its Orientation (what we in the trade call the Greater Bad), it's permitted and authorised to keep you more or less intact for as long as you're useful. So; They're pretty damn strong. Except—

Except we're stronger. Not you; me, and my kind, adepts, those of us with the Knack. To us is granted the privilege of a greater strength; on us is laid the burden of using it to keep you lot safe. I can winkle out one of Them as easily as you pick a caterpillar off a cabbage leaf, except that it's not quite as simple as that. Think about weeding onions. You pull up the weed and the onion comes with it, because the weed has cunningly wrapped and entwined its roots round the onion's, to persuade you and me to leave it alone. So, I can yank the unwelcome visitor out of your head easy as winking, but there may not be much of you left afterwards. Or I can carefully and patiently untangle its roots and suckers, a delicate and exhausting process which can sometimes take me a whole second (that's a *very* long time, in context) and remove it without significant permanent damage. *I* can; as I may already have mentioned, I'm very good at this stuff. Some of my colleagues aren't quite so proficient, though what they lack in finesse they tend to make up in zeal, and you can track their progress through the provinces by counting all the people who spend all day sitting dead still and being fed through straws.

We're stronger; that's it, that's all. By this point, my third-years will have heard an awful lot of bullshit about Good and Evil, but that's strictly for the paying customers. Fact; we're stronger. Period.

Stronger; except—

The crick in my neck was the least of my problems. Being inside someone's head— You'd think I'd get used to it, eventually, but you don't. Actually, it gradually gets worse. Immediately afterwards, it's fine. If anything, you get a slight buzz, say a brandy and a half's worth, which lasts for up to an hour. But then you find yourself feeling a bit tired and sleepy, so you retire to your quarters and take a nap; and when you wake up— People who've had mountain fever and survived tell you about the weariness, the dull ache in every bone, the iron-wedge-splitting headache, the way it takes every last scrap of your strength to scratch your ear or keep your eyelids apart. A bit like that, but the physical stuff isn't really so bad. It's the feeling of having had something solid, cold and intensely serrated shoved right up your consciousness that I don't like. And that was after a relatively civilised encounter with someone (all right, something) I've come to consider a friend.

Stronger my arse. We do it because we're obliged to, but it's not easy.

But the crick in the neck was *additional,* and entirely the fault of the people of Sabades for having such lousy inns, so I felt and resented it rather more keenly than the actual discomfort merited. You go to a place, you put yourself through all that, entirely for their sakes, and how do they thank you? By housing you in crummy inns with nasty cramped beds and stinking beer. True, the *Diamonds* was built four hundred years ago, but the least they could do, surely, is pull it down and replace it with something better, just in case I ever need to stay there.

Accordingly, I wasn't at my fizziest. The last thing I wanted to see was myself, slumped against the wall with my head lolling and my neck snapped.

Nuts, I thought.

Also; the lady has a temper, for all her demure and dignified demeanour. *Instar hominis* is such a harmless little Form, useful and inoffensive. I do it the simple way. I pull out a hair and mumble the words under my breath, and the hair turns into a tiny little copy of me, too small to be seen (but an adept can smell it; a really, really sensitive one); the little tiny me hangs discreetly around, gathering information, then makes its way back to me and tells me what it's found out before popping conveniently out of existence.

She must have a nose like a spaniel, I thought. Also the strength to catch my diminutive observer, expand it to full size, wring its neck and transport it back through either a bolted door, two feet of dense thatch or a solid wall. Not sure I could do that. Not just strong, I said to myself; stronger.

Not that it mattered, because she wasn't my fault. Maybe in Idalia they have different attitudes to privacy and professional etiquette, as well as four testicles, we simply don't know. In any event, I intended to be on the first coach out of Sabades, and with any luck I'd never see or hear about her again.

You can guess what happened, can't you?

I WAS ACTUALLY on the coach, with my luggage on the roof and my feet up on the seat opposite, next stop Boethia. I was vaguely wondering why we weren't moving yet, and wondering what the voices whose words I couldn't quite make out were saying.

The door opened and a helmeted head appeared. Men in helmets are always bad news. "Everybody out," said the helmeted head.

I looked at him. "Excuse me?"

"Out," he said.

Define strength. I could turn him into a cockroach in a heartbeat with no effort at all. He had the full authority of the State behind him. In theory I have benefit of clergy, which makes me even stronger than the State, but invoking the privilege would involve endless bureaucracy, form-filling and faffing-about, and I'd get a ferocious telling-off from my superiors for annoying the civil authorities. So that made him stronger, on that occasion, from my perspective. "Just coming," I said.

My left foot had gone to sleep. Pins and needles. I despise pain. The coachman was getting my luggage down off the roof. "What am I supposed to have done?" I asked.

The soldier wasn't looking at me. "Nothing," he said. "But all coaches out of the city are cancelled, because of the murder."

"What murder?"

25

THERE'S NO PRIORY in Sabades Amar, but they have a prior; don't ask. The prior is the third most important official in the regional administration, which if you ask me is a bit like being the third biggest flea on a blind fiddler's dog, but the Sabadeans care about shit like that, and why not?

Correction; they had a prior. Not anymore. Some scoundrel had crawled in through a window and stabbed him in the ear as he slept. Eyewitnesses reported seeing someone scrambling out of a window in the prior's apartments just before a chambermaid came in and discovered the body. The suspect was described as female, young, straight black hair, rather nice-looking, wearing a sort of white sheet getup secured at the shoulder with a distinctive-looking brooch.

For crying out loud, I thought. Still, none of my business. We don't interfere in the operation of the civil authorities. Three cheers for the doctrine of separation of powers.

Still, it explained why she'd been so rough with my *instar hominis*. I gave the matter a very small amount of thought and came to the conclusion, on minimal evidence, that if she'd killed the prior, the prior probably needed killing, and went back to the *Flawless Diamonds* to see if I could hire a cart of some kind to take me to Boethia. Guess who I saw, the moment I walked through the door.

"They're looking for you," I said, trying to keep my voice down.

She yawned and poured tea into a bowl. "You again," she said. "Who and why?"

"They think you murdered the prior."

"What's a prior?"

It occurred to me to wonder how come an Idalian could speak flawless idiomatic Robur. The various hypotheses that sprang to mind were all very well, but if so, how come she didn't know what prior meant? "Did you or didn't you?"

She gave me dazzling smile. "Did you know," she said, "that your breath doesn't smell very nice?"

Her mind was still that insipid shade of beige. "Tough," I said. "Look, I don't give a damn if you've murdered twenty priors. But unless you enjoy talking to policemen, I suggest you get out of sight. Out of town would be better, but I don't think that would be possible right now."

"Sweet of you to be concerned, but what business is it of yours?"

"None whatsoever. Silly of me not to have thought of that earlier. Goodbye."

I stood up, headed for the door, got three paces and stopped dead. Stronger, I thought. "Hey," I said.

"Come back here and sit down."

I felt her let me go. Eight paces to the door. The hell with it, I thought, and went back to her table. "You're starting to annoy me," I said.

"Oh dear, how sad. Who did you say is looking for me?"

"Everybody."

She nodded thoughtfully. "That's a nuisance," she said. "Do they really think I killed somebody?"

"A woman fitting your description was seen leaving the scene of the crime," I said.

"There must be loads of women like me in this town."

"No," I said.

"Ah." She nodded. "That's awkward. You'd better find me somewhere to hide."

"Now just a—"

Definitely stronger. It was like a giant hand cupped over my head; thumb in one ear, little finger in the other, two fingers in my eyes, and my skull slightly more fragile than an egg. "Please," she added.

"Sorry," I said, trying hard not to gasp my words. "Don't think I caught that last bit."

"Please?"

"Since you ask so nicely."

She let go. I gave her *vertex fulminis*, right between the eyes. She wobbled. I caught hold of her shoulder to keep her from falling backwards onto the floor. Stronger, then, but not impossibly so.

"Now we've got that over with," I said, "tell me. Did you kill the prior or not?"

"That *hurt*."

"The slow dripping noise is my heart bleeding. Did you or didn't you?"

"Oh all right. If you must know, yes, I did."

"You murdered the *prior*—"

"Would you mind terribly much not shouting quite so loud?"

Fine, I thought, and plunged into her head.

28

YOU'RE REALLY NOT supposed to do that. It can cause serious damage to both the plunger and the plunged, it's completely unethical and extremely bad manners. At least, it's all that where I come from. Who knows? In Idalia, it could be the equivalent of shaking hands.

She hadn't expected it. I landed on my feet, stood up and looked round. The usual; marble floor, tapestries, oil lamps, log fire. Just for once, I wished it didn't have to be quite so subjective. "Hello?" I called out. "Anybody home?"

She appeared, sitting in an armchair. "That's rude," she said. "How did you do that?"

I stood over her and put my hands round her throat. I didn't squeeze, not really. "Why did you kill the prior?"

"It all feels very real. Is this an illusion or are you really here?"

I squeezed. My hands passed through her neck and met. "Please?" I said.

The tapestries, I noticed, were neither red nor blue; a sort of soothingly bland beige colour. "Sorry," she said, "I'm not allowed to tell you. Rules. You know how it is."

I let go. "Why did you kill a prior when you don't even know what a prior is?"

"Can't tell you. Sorry."

"Why did you come all this way to kill someone who couldn't possibly have any relevance to you? How did you even know about him in the first place?"

"I'm going to count to three," she said. "One."

"Answer me and I'll find you somewhere to hide."

She put her head on one side, like a puzzled dog. "Getting involved is a high price to pay for curiosity."

Yes, I thought, it is. And I suddenly remembered that it was none of my business. Except—

"You answer my question. I find you somewhere to hide. I then go away and have nothing more to do with you, ever again."

She thought about it. "Oh, go on, then. But the hiding place first, I think."

"You don't trust—"

"No."

Fine. Well, I wouldn't trust me. I never have and, please God, I never will. "Round the back of this horrible building is a shed. In the middle of the floor, under a pile of mouldy and evil-smelling sacks, is a trapdoor, leading to an old root cellar. It's dark, damp and full of the most enormous spiders, but nobody knows about it except one of the local organised crime syndicates. You're welcome," I added, to save her the bother of thanking me. "Now then. Why are you here and why did you kill the prior?"

She pursed her lips. "You want the truth?"

"Yes."

"I don't know."

All around me, everything—walls, floor, ceiling—turned blue. The truth. Marvellous. "You don't know."

"I wasn't told, no."

"But that doesn't make sense. Why would anybody—?"

"Two."

Believe it or not, there's quite a substantial literature on the strategic and tactical considerations involved in fighting someone inside his or her own head. The consensus is that where the combatants are evenly matched in skill and resources, the odds are overwhelmingly against the intruder. Screw it, I thought. Absolutely none of my business. "Fine," I said. "Enjoy the spiders. It was a real pleasure meeting you."

"Fibber."

I slipped out, wiping my metaphorical feet on the metaphorical mat as I left. She smiled at me. "Round the back, you said."

I nodded. "If I were you," I said, "I'd give it at least a week. The watch in this town is very conscientious."

She stood up. "Noted," she said. "Goodbye."

I TRIED EVERYWHERE I knew, but nobody was hiring carts or horses. Finally, when I dropped in at the *Transfigured by Joy*, I found a watch sergeant and two steelnecks waiting for me. They were interested in knowing why I was so very anxious to leave town. I told them I was a busy man on a schedule and I needed to be somewhere else, which was true. They gave me that don't-do-it-again look that law enforcement loves to bestow on the innocent, and went out, leaving me to pay for their drinks.

Stuck in horrible Sabades Amar. They'd even stopped the mail, so I couldn't write to our people in Drutz to tell them I'd be late. I sat down on a step outside the

Guildhall, so fed up and frustrated I could hardly think, and tried to pull myself together.

None, I told myself, of my business. But I had nothing else to do, and the problem was bothering me, like a fibre of bacon caught between two back teeth.

Well now, I thought. A woman, a female adept of all the impossible things, sets out from Idalia, a faraway country of which we know little, and comes all the way across the world to a hick town in the Ozidan peninsula. She says she doesn't know what a prior is, and I believe her, but she kills one nonetheless. Not something you'd do lightly, or on a whim. There are people in this world who stab other people for fun, but they generally tend to do it out in the street, and their victims are close by and handy. To get inside the prior's lodging, armed with a knife, would call for skill, ice in the veins and above all, patience; not characteristics you associate with street-stabbing crazies. Makes no *sense*—

Except—

Let's suppose killing the prior wasn't the reason she came here. Let's suppose that the bloody purpose was part of someone else's agenda, and she was co-opted—why? Because she's from out of town, as far out of town as it's possible to get. I thought about that. Still made no sense, except—

Demonic possession. Put that into the mix, and potential sense comes gushing out. Maybe Idalians, or Idalian adepts, or Idalian females, or Idalian female adepts are really easy to possess; more likely, the fact that she could have no possible motive was the whole point. To make it really, really mysterious. Or to make sure that no interested party could hijack the murder to suit their own purposes—to make trouble, put the blame on some blameless faction, cause a riot, start a war. Neat as ninepence, and just the sort of clear, sensible thinking I've come to expect from the smarter elements of the Loyal Opposition. Let's do this thing, because it's necessary, but let's try and make sure nobody else gets hurt. The sort of thinking I've stopped expecting from my side of the fence, because I don't react well to disappointment.

Except—

If she'd been possessed when I met her the first time I'd have smelt it on her, sure as eggs (unless I couldn't because she was Idalian, but for crying out loud let's not overcomplicate matters). So she'd have had to have been nobbled at some point between parting from me and the murder. During that rather narrow timeframe, an agent of the opposite Orientation would have had to notice her, figure out the advantages in using her, draw up a plan of action, get it approved by Area Command and signed off by Division, then slid into her head without her noticing. A bit tight, but possible.

Except that since the murder, I'd been in her head myself, and if one of Them had been in there at any point during the last two years, the smell would've been strong enough to bring me out in a rash. You can tell, believe me. Unless it's different with Idalians, Idalian adepts, Idalian females, Idalian female adepts, Idalian female adepts during the third week after Ascension—

If only the coaches were running, I'd be miles away by now and something else would be nagging away at me, eating into my brain like a beetle, instead of this; something I could eventually solve, quite likely. I think I already told you how much I loathe mysteries.

Demonic possession. Just as well I know somebody who's something of an authority on the subject.

THE CORN-CHANDLER FROM Obergallen was in the Corn Exchange, presumably chandling a spot of corn. I sidled up next to him and slithered in through his ear.

"Now what?" said my old pal.

"You were about to tell me something," I said.

I know him quite well. Like most of his kind, he's hopeless at lying. The rule is, to bring us to our harm, the instruments of darkness tell us truths; fibbing is, strictly speaking, against the rules, or at least a misdemeanour violation of the code of conduct. When my pal lies he goes a rather garish shade of lemon. "No, I don't think so," he said.

"Yes," I said. "You were."

"No."

"Yes." I put on my stern expression, designed to imply that even though we were pals, I was still an officer of the ecclesiastical court. It cuts no ice with him, goes without saying, but it does convey the fact that I seriously want to know. "Don't make me give you a direct order."

"Idiot." He sighed. "Why should I tell you what you know already?"

"Come again?"

"Oh please." He scowled at me. "I can smell her on you."

Ah.

"That bloody woman." He doesn't usually swear. Another code violation. "Keep her the hell away from me, you hear me?"

"You've met her."

"Oh yes."

Made no sense. My pal already had a host. He's not given to outbursts of initiative, and his superiors have a realistic opinion of his capabilities. Therefore he wouldn't be chosen for anything difficult or complicated. "She's Idalian," I said.

"I know."

"What's she doing in Ozidan?"

He shuddered. "Don't mess me around, please," he said. "I've had about as much as I can handle today, thank you ever so much. And any minute now I'm going to have those pinheads from Divisional Command down on me like a ton of bricks, and it's not my *fault*." He paused and took a deep breath. "Look, I know it's not your fault either, you're just a footslogger like me, but it really is too bad. I mean, what's got into you people, letting something like that roam about loose in a public place? It's bloody irresponsible, is what it is. You ought to be ashamed of yourselves."

Strong words. "I have no idea what you're talking about."

Apparently I go green when I lie. He looked at me. I guess I wasn't green. "Straight up?"

"Cross my heart and hope to die in a cellarful of rats."
"You're kidding me. You don't *know?*"
"Not unless you tell me."
"Oh for pity's sake. You people—"
"*Tell me.*"
He blinked, took a deep breath and vanished.

WHICH ISN'T POSSIBLE. They can't just disappear. I'm not talking about invisibility. Inside someone's head, you see with the inner eye, so conjuring tricks are completely beside the point. If I couldn't see him, he was no longer there. I was alone with the slow, unimaginably mundane ruminations of the corn-chandler. What the hell?

I left quickly, hung around the corn exchange for a few minutes to see if anybody there was acting oddly, then made my way back to the *Transfigured by Joy,* where they do a six-stuiver stockfish casserole that tastes remarkably like leaf mould.

More to think about. Clearly my pal had encountered her, and equally clearly it hadn't been a pleasant experience for him. Now, unless the inside of her head had seen more recent footfall than a beer tent on market day, one consequence of their encounter must have been a dead prior. I have to say that in my experience, my pal isn't like that. He's a conscientious officer and he obeys orders when absolutely necessary, but spectacular acts of violence aren't his usual MO. It's not that he's squeamish exactly. He says that the toxins released into the host's system by shock, rage and bloodlust give him indigestion. Besides, he'd said something about Division being down on him like a ton of bricks, so presumably he hadn't been ordered to kill any priors. His lot are very careful not to do any unauthorised evil, for moral-high-ground purposes. Logical conclusion, therefore; he'd been inside her mind and together they'd murdered the prior, but he *hadn't wanted to*—

Made no sense.

Unfortunately, it was starting to look annoyingly like my business after all. He was, after all, a contact, a business associate, I'd go so far as to say a colleague. Whatever it was she'd done to him had left him traumatised, and now he'd simply disappeared, something which is, of course, impossible. No actual harm could come to him. Could it? I realised I had no idea. You can't kill them, in the same way you can't kill Thursday or symmetry or an angle of forty-five degrees. You can hurt them. They have a pain threshold so low it's practically a pain cellar. But you can't damage them in any permanent way, any more than you can cut up water with scissors. At least, as far as we know. It was, of course, entirely possible that they knew how to kill them stone dead in Idalia.

Screw it, I thought. In the normal course of events I'm as reluctant to get involved as a cat is to go outside in the rain, but I'm also a qualified practitioner, an officer of the ecclesiastical court, an honorary canon juridical and (nominally at least) one of the good guys. Nor could I plead a previous engagement, since I couldn't get out of bloody Sabades unless I walked. Also the small matter of what might get said to me if it transpired that something very big and very bad had happened when I was right there on the spot and I'd done absolutely nothing about it. Nuts, I thought.

So I WENT to the root cellar out back of the *Flawless Diamonds*. She wasn't there.

Deep breath. These things are sent to try us. Time for me to do my celebrated impression of a spaniel.

Tracking someone by scent alone isn't nearly as easy as it sounds. Quite apart from the funny looks you get, it's tiring. All that sniffing gives me a headache, and I bump into things. It could have been worse, though. The scent was reasonably fresh and the trail didn't take me too close to any tanneries, dye works, linen yards or other strongly-scented operations, so I managed not to lose it. Instead, I found myself standing in the middle of Horsefair looking at the main gate of the Watch house. Marvellous.

Justice in Sabades Amar is many things, but it's not long drawn out. The average turnaround time between the first hand on the collar and the swish of the headsman's axe is twenty-four hours, and when they want to, they can really get a move on. I figured the murder of the prior would be fairly close to the top of their list of, no pun intended, priorities. There would, of course, be a trial. The Sabadois aren't barbarians. But their idea of the burden of proof is a sworn affidavit from the district procurator. If I wanted to do anything, I'd have to do it quickly. I barged in through the door and asked for the duty officer.

"I want to see the prisoner," I said.

He looked at me. "Which one? We've got a hundred and six."

"The girl who killed the prior."

He smiled at me. "In your dreams," he said.

Oh well. I'm not supposed to do that sort of thing, but what the hell. In through his nose, up the eustachian tube into his brain, a quick flick of the wrists to jerk his centre of volition through a hundred and eighty degrees. "In the circumstances," he said, "you can have ten minutes."

"Thank you," I said politely.

They'd put her in my old cell. Years ago, a silly misunderstanding, I won't bother you with the details, but the stone I'd loosened with the stub end of a spoon had been mortared back into place, going to show how sharp and on-the-ball they are in Sabades. It's the very last cell at the end of a very long passageway leading nowhere, with loads of doors and guards to get past coming or going. Just the thought of it made my teeth ache.

She lifted her head. "You," she said.

I waited till the door clanged shut. "They got you, then."

"Yes. Of all the stupid—"

I raised my hand. "Let's not go into all that now," I said. "Would you like me to get you out of here?"

She scowled at me. "You honestly think you can do that."

I nodded. "Given your abilities," I said, "I'm surprised to find you still here."

"What's that supposed to mean?"

It occurred to me how little I knew about Idalian adepts. "Couldn't you have just—well, you know?"

"What?"

"Nudged their minds? Just a little?"

"What are you talking about?"

Idalia, I thought, a faraway place, et cetera. "Leave this to me," I said, and banged on the door with my fist.

Smugness, I'm told, doesn't become me. I wouldn't know. In the usual course of events, I have so very little to be smug about. This time, though; by the time we walked out of the Watch house, with the duty officer opening the door for us and apologising for any inconvenience, I felt as tight-chested as a bullfrog.

"Back home," she said to me, "if I did that, they'd cut me open and wind out my guts on a stick."

"Against the rules?"

"It'd be unthinkable."

"And in about half an hour you'd have been dead. Must you whine about absolutely everything?"

She gave me a look that should have scoured me down to the bone. Oddly enough, it didn't. "If I'd known what you were going to do, I wouldn't have let you."

"Fine," I said. "Go back. I'm not stopping you."

I honestly believe she considered it, for about two seconds. A very long time, in context. "So that's it, is it? I'm off the hook."

"Hardly," I said. "In an hour or so they'll snap out of it and wonder where in hell you can have got to. So that's all right. You can appease your violated conscience by letting them catch you and everything will be just dandy. In the meantime, however, you can tell me what you did to my friend."

"What friend?"

I realised I needed to choose my words carefully. "Not friend," I said. "Associate. You see, for reasons I'm not authorised to disclose, I have a sort of a business relationship with the demon who was in your mind earlier today—"

"The what?"

WE GO WAY back, my pal and I. I first ran into him when I was still in third year. As part of the course, we had to do a certain amount of practical fieldwork—sounds good, doesn't it? Get the kids away from their books for an afternoon, give them a taste of what's waiting for them out there in the big, wide world, they'll thank you for it in the long run. Great idea. What it meant in practice was a bunch of semi-trained, grass-green idiots roaming through the streets of a major city, scared out of their wits and looking for the worst possible sort of trouble.

Some of them found it. My friend Maxentiolus, for example. His assignment was to locate and cast out an evil spirit. He passed the theory with flying colours, ninety-eight per cent, the highest grade ever recorded up to that time in a mid-term assessment. His tutors declared that he knew more about all that stuff than they did and he was equipped to deal with any situation he might happen to encounter out there on the street. So off he went, wrapped up in his woolly muffler because he had a weak chest and his mother worried about him, to do battle with the Prince of Darkness. Afterwards, at the memorial service in the Rose Chapel, I overheard two of our tutors speculating about what could have gone wrong, and the conclusion they arrived at was that poor little Maxentiolus had run into a problem comprised in the two per cent of the syllabus he hadn't learned by heart. Moral: stuff happens.

Mercifully, on the occasion of my first real-life encounter with the opposite Orientation, it didn't happen to me. I'd been given exactly the same assignment as poor Max, and I'd seen what happened to him; in fact I was there when he jumped, and heard the unforgettable sound of a human body hitting a stone-flagged courtyard after falling from a hundred-foot tower. A week later, when I walked across the Old Flower Market and caught that faint but distinctive scent, I wasn't at my chirpiest, oddly enough.

I'd chosen the flower market because, in the mid-term practicals, failure is acceptable under certain circumstances. One of them is being sent to find a demon but there aren't any demons about. Fair enough; everybody has a blank day sometimes, and as we know, there's only a couple of hundred thousand of the critters in all of Creation. Just now I chose my words with care; faint but distinctive. You have to be quite close to pick up the scent. If, all things considered, you feel it's not in your best interests to pick up a scent, there's no better place in the city than the flower market, which stinks to high heaven of flowers to the point where you can hardly breathe.

So what? I cheat. But I'm also fundamentally honest. I'd done my very best not to run across a demon, but if I did locate one, I couldn't just walk on by as though it wasn't there. And, sure enough, as I strolled past a stall selling roasted chestnuts, there it was, rank as a fox.

The lecturers tell you—I give this lecture myself once a year, and I describe it this way. A demon smells like nothing else. I can't be more specific than that, because it's entirely subjective. The same demon will smell musty-puky-mouldy to me and oily-shitty-rotten to you and faintly of eglantine to someone else. But the smell will be literally indescribable and absolutely unlike anything else you've ever encountered. And that's how you know.

I stopped and looked round, and there was this woman, tying violets into bundles. She was the absolute Saloninan ideal of nondescript; not smart, not shabby, any age between thirty-five and seventy, small, clean, unbleached linen smock, pepper-and-salt hair, the sort of woman who gets run over by a cart in broad daylight because she's so ordinary she's invisible. I felt in my pocket and found a twenty-stuiver, the only coin I'd got. "A bunch of violets, please," I said, and offered her the coin.

She looked up at me, then at the money. "Sorry," she said. "I haven't got change for that."

I saw him behind her eyes. "Don't worry about it," I said, and sort of prodded towards her with the coin.

These days I don't need to bother with it, but the easiest way for novices is simultaneous physical touch and eye-contact. It practically makes the connection for you, and then in you go. She opened her mouth to say thank you or something like that, and I dived in between her parted lips like a rat up a drain. It's a small miracle I didn't give her the horrors, but somehow or other I got away with it; and there I was, inside a stranger's mind for the first time ever.

A stranger's, mark you. I'd been inside my tutors so often I'd practically beaten a path, like cows to the barn. It suddenly occurred to me that here I was, *on active service*—no longer among friends, the swords don't have buttons on the points, if you get in trouble you can't call a halt and ask if you can start again from the beginning. Extraordinary feeling, that. It's like coming out of a small, dark house into searingly bright sunshine. I imagine it's how it feels hatching from an egg. The first thing you register is sheer terror; and then you remember that you're not exactly naked and helpless, you do have certain skills and weapons; above all, you remember (though it's hard to accept and get your head around) that you're supposed to be a *predator*—

All policemen are predators, after all. Laws are for statesmen, justice is for judges, but their, sorry, our job is to track down, outrun and bring down our legitimate, terrified prey. When the captured animal turns, struggling madly under your claws, and asks you; what business is it of yours, what harm did I ever do you—? There are plenty of easy answers, which I teach to my students. For the public good, to keep people safe, to punish crime, to uphold our shared values as a society, to fight Evil. There's a certain amount of truth in answers like that, just as there's a certain amount of silver in Duke Aimeric's ninety-nine-per-cent-copper silver dollars; just enough silver to cover the copper completely, so that nobody sees it until it's too late.

Anyway, there he was. He looked at me. I looked at him. "Oh for crying out loud," he said.

"Get out," I shouted. "Get *out!*"

He gave me a hurt look. "Keep your hair on," he said. "I'm going as fast as I can."

"Get out of here right now."

"I can't."

This is it, I thought. I gathered my intellectual and spiritual weapons around me, and knew they were good; sharp, strong and in perfect working order. "Really," I drawled. "Why not?"

"You're standing in the way."

Good point. My mind began to teem with tactical and strategic considerations. If I stood to one side, would I be offering a vulnerable flank to a sudden, lightning-fast attack? If I stepped back, would I give him the distance he needed for a full-on lunge? I realised I couldn't move without completely compromising my entire defence. But if I stayed where I was, he couldn't leave. "Turn around," I said.

"Why?"

So that I could rabbit-punch him, snap his neck and hurl his paralysed body out of the nearest ear, just to be on the safe side. "Because I say so," I said.

"You're new at this, aren't you?"

I took a deep breath. "Yup," I said. "So my techniques are absolutely up to date and cutting edge. You want to try anything, be my guest. Go ahead, make my day."

He sighed. "You've got yourself stuck, haven't you?"

I made a sort of growling noise, which he interpreted quite accurately. "Tell you what," he said, "how about this? You go out and come back in again, and this time I'll be over there, so when I leave you'll have me on your right side and you'll be perfectly safe from any known form of sneak attack. How does that sound?"

I thought about it. I happen to have a brilliant tactical mind. I considered all the possibilities, the potential traps, ambushes, stratagems and gambits. "Thanks," I said, and backed out they way I'd come.

When I came in again, he was exactly where he'd said he'd be, hands spread wide to show good faith. "Ready?" he said.

"Yes."

"I'll be going, then. Good luck with your future career."

"Thanks."

He left. I spent a whole real-time second inspecting the inside of the violet-seller's head for hidden mines and booby-traps. Nothing. Then I got out, just in time to avoid causing a major haemorrhage.

46

"Demon," I said. "Oh come *on*. The little horror who got inside you and made you kill the fucking prior."

She looked at me. "Is a fucking prior different from an ordinary one?"

I closed my eyes. There are times when I wish I'd gone into my brother-in-law's carpet business in Mondesir.

"Only," she went on, "I thought all your clergy were supposed to take a vow of celibacy. Or is that just a traveller's tale, like the big feet? It does sound rather odd, if you ask me. It's not like that at home. Of course we don't have priests, as such. Are you celibate?"

I timed it just right. I stepped directly in front of her, so she couldn't help tripping over the back of my heel. I helped her on her way with a very gentle shove with the flat of my hand in the small of her back. She went straight down, and anyone watching would be sure that all they'd seen was some woman slip and fall in the street, and the man she was with help her up again.

I had her arm twisted behind her back. "This way," I said.

Down an alley, in through the gates of a tannery, long since abandoned and derelict for non-payment of taxes. She was still dizzy from the fall, and I filled her mind with the buzzing of angry wasps so she couldn't think. All the movable plant was stripped out years ago, but the vats are still there, full to the brim with stinking black water. I pushed her to her knees and held her nose an inch above the meniscus. "Tell me what you did to my friend," I said. "Please."

I realised I'd got myself stuck again. I didn't dare let up on the wasps, but while they were buzzing inside her head she couldn't think, and if she couldn't think she couldn't answer my question. Stupid. "Tell you what," I said. "I'll let you go, and we'll start again. All right?"

Her head moved under my hand, which I took for a nod, meaning acquiescence. I let go and withdrew the wasps. Something hit me so hard I nearly blacked out, and I fell in the tanning vat.

I made the mistake of opening my eyes. Whatever was in the vat stung them like hell. I felt her foot on the top of my head, pushing me under. I swathed myself with *lorica* to keep the foul water out of my mouth and nose and lashed out at her with *mundus vergens*. I heard a thump, which probably meant I'd knocked her off her feet. I pulled myself together and clambered out of the vat.

She was lying on her side, one arm up to the elbow in stinking black water. I stood over her and nudged her in the ribs with my toe. "We'll call that a draw," I said. "Now can we start again?"

"Piss off."

I held out my hand. She grabbed it and got to her feet. Her white dress was covered in grimy black splashes. There was a cut on her forehead, either from *mundus* or where she'd hit the stone floor. "What did you do to my friend?"

She sighed. "I'm filthy," she said, "and it's all your fault."

"You started it."

"No I didn't."

"Yes you did," I said, "By doing whatever it was you did to my friend. What was that, by the way?"

She sat down on the floor, with her knees drawn up under her chin. "You don't smell very nice," she said.

"Neither do you. Now, are you going to answer me or do we have to do more fighting?"

"What was that thing you hit me with?"

"Answer the question. Please."

She looked at me, and brushed a wisp of hair out of her mouth. "There's a war in my country," she said. "I was sent here to get weapons."

I nodded slowly. "I guess we're not talking about bits of metal."

"No. It's not that sort of war."

My head was hurting. "Let me guess," I said. "You don't have demons in Idalia."

"Is that what you call them? What are they?"

Oh boy. "Tell me," I said, "about the war."

So she told me.

Idalia (she told me) isn't like here. Not to put too fine a point on it, it's different, in a lot of ways. In fact, the only way she was able to cope with being in a place so shockingly, nauseatingly different was to flood her mind and soul with *qin*—don't ask, she said quickly, it's an ectoplasmic discharge generated inside the liver and diffused throughout the various bodily, mental and spiritual systems by means of extreme meditation, and it has powerful narcotic and anaesthetic qualities, but after a bit it makes you feel sick as a dog and extremely ratty. I wasn't helping either, she added. She thought I ought to know that.

49

Idalia is ruled by its adepts, just over half of whom are female. They provide for all the needs of the non-adept population, using *jia* (again, don't ask) and in return they receive adulation, worship and unquestioning obedience. The adepts are, needless to say, all thoroughly enlightened philosopher-kings and queens whose only interest is pure science and the pursuit of truth and beauty, but very occasionally a difference of opinion arises over some fine point of aesthetics or academic protocol, and then all hell breaks loose. War is probably a misleading term, since there aren't any armies as such, no campaigns or pitched battles. For one thing, a single extra-smart adept can easily defeat a whole army of only slightly less smart opponents. Furthermore, in such a highly nuanced society of more-or-less equals, it's incredibly rare to find two people who think precisely the same way about any issue, so sides and alliances are as fluid as floodwater. It's more a sort of general free-for-all which goes on for a very long time, after which the survivors move two hundred miles east and start building new cities. It's just as well that Idalia is such a big place and so sparsely populated, because huge bits of it are so badly compromised that nothing will ever grow there again, and just being downwind of it brings you out in the most appalling rash.

"So what we need," she said, "is a new weapon."

"Really?"

"Yes," she said gravely. "A weapon so powerful that it'll make war unthinkable."

"Oh," I said. "One of those."

She gave me a sour look. "If we've got a really power-ful weapon, everyone else will know they simply don't stand a chance, and then there won't be any more of these stupid wars. Which is why I came here."

I frowned. "No disrespect," I said, "but I think you're probably wasting your time. We haven't got anything like that here. The craft—" I hesitated. "We call it that, but really it doesn't sound anything like what you've got in Idalia. We've got a few Forms, like the one I bashed you with, but by the sound of it, you've got heavy artillery."

"You may not think of it as a weapon," she said. "After all, a weapon's just a tool put to a particular use. A less advanced society, like yours, may well not realise the military capability of what you've got." She paused for a moment. "That *thing*—"

"Ah."

She took a deep breath. "We heard about it from the Tace, who heard about it from the Lourenshabat, who heard about it from the Echmen. They said, over here there are creatures that can crawl inside a person's mind and control them, make them do what you want. To us, that's a weapon. That's the sort of weapon that could put a stop to war for ever and ever."

I looked at her. "Let me stop you there," I said.

THE SECOND TIME I met him was about six months later. I was about to take my final exams. I wasn't in the most cheerful frame of mind, because what with one thing and another I hadn't got around to doing very much of the work I was supposed to have done, and my chances of passing were slim. They hold Finals in a large room on the third floor of the Old Tower, and the thing you immediately notice about it is that it's circular. No corners. No place, in other words, to hide. It's a stark and simple metaphor. You can bluff your way through tutorials and the practicals, but when they read out the questions and you're alone at your desk facing a sheet of paper as blank and bottomless as the Eastern ocean, if you haven't got the right stuff you're screwed.

I'd made up my mind that my only hope was to get a hundred per cent on my practicals, which might just earn me a viva if I was really lucky. Therefore I had to get out there and practice, in the hope that I'd find something to practice on. This was, of course, strictly against the rules. An unqualified adept isn't allowed to go prowling solo through the streets perfecting his skills on the public. There's got to be proper supervision, backup, support teams, lawyers. I knew I'd be breaching the Studium's charter and risking an unfortunate incident with the civil authorities, as well as lives, sanities and souls. But it was that or lose a whole year, so what could I do?

I got lucky in the third bar I went into, the old *Fortitude & Temperance* down by the pig market. There was an old man slumped in the corner. He had vomit down his front and round the corners of his mouth, and he was talking to himself in a low murmur. The quart jug in front of him was full. I paused and sniffed. Just perceptible over the stink of booze and sick, a different smell that made the others seem like roses. Hello, I thought, and popped in for a look.

"You again."

Trying to describe the way I perceive them is like trying to describe a rainbow to a man blind from birth, but here goes. Imagine that you get exactly the same quantity and quality of information from a smell as you do from sight. I guess that's what dogs do. I could describe him to you in perfect and minute detail, except human vocabulary doesn't have the right words. I perceive everything about them—height, weight, build, manner, characteristics, even character—in terms of subtle graduations and calibrations of scent. Once you get used to it, it's easy. In fact, you can understand a fellow creature far more precisely and accurately that way than you can with just sight and hearing.

"Small world," I said. "Out."

He slumped. I'd caught him in the middle of what, for want of a better word, I guess I'll have to call his dinner. He was going through his host's memories, absorbing them as coherent narrative and excreting them as a dream, which was why the host was mumbling and screwing up his eyes. I saw him find his father hanging in the barn when he was twelve, my pal's idea of a savoury.

"Just a minute," he said. "Have you got your ticket yet?"

"Didn't you hear me? I told you to get out. Now."

He relaxed. "You haven't, have you? You're still at school."

I had no face in there, but I could feel myself go red. "Makes no difference. I have the power."

"Yup." He grinned. "But you're not allowed to use it."

I could feel command of the situation slipping away like a tide going out. "Doesn't matter. That's between me and the authorities."

"So you really don't care if I lodge an official complaint. Before you've even qualified. That's not going to look good, is it?"

I had the power to shred him into ribbons, each ribbon curled by pain into a spiral. "You wouldn't."

"Oh come on, we're supposed to be *enemies.*" He beamed at me. "You clown," he said.

All around him, the old man's mother was dying of cholera. "Can you turn that down?" I asked him.

"What? Oh, right. I forgot, your lot are so squeamish." The memory faded. "Of course you are, you've got so much to be squeamish about. And yes, of course I'll go quietly. I was just yanking your chain."

I felt my anger dribble away, taking my fear with it. "Thanks," I said.

He stayed where he was, looking at me as though there was a bit of me missing, but he wasn't sure which one. "So what's a third-year doing playing at being a field grade? There's got to be a reason."

"Fighting evil is my vocation."

He made a sniggering noise. "Apart from that."

So I told him. Don't ask me why. Maybe he tempted me. Or maybe it was simply because I'd been worrying myself sick for such a long time, and there was nobody I could talk to. He listened patiently, then said, "I can see why you're all stressed out. Three years down the toilet, and then you've got to go home and explain to your old man. Serves you right, of course. You shouldn't have left it all to the last minute."

"I'd sort of gathered that."

"Still." He thought for a moment. "I could help you."

"Oh please," I said. "Do I look like I was born stupid?"

"Free of charge," he said, "no obligation."

"Oh sure."

"No." He looked at me quite intensely. "Subverting the inner workings of your order is definitely part of my job description. And helping you cheat on your exam qualifies as subversion. And I'm not exactly rushed off my feet right now, so I might as well be doing that as something else. It'd be fun."

Well. I was pretty desperate. "Right," I said. "And all I have to do is sign a bit of paper giving you my soul in return. No thanks."

He looked hurt. "I said, no obligation. This would be a freebie, one time only, as a gesture of solidarity from one bone-idle self-indulgent under-achiever to another. Nobody will ever know. Well, what about it?"

He was looking straight at me, and in his eyes I thought I could see my father's face when I told him the reason why I'd failed the exam. "You can't help me," I said. "What are you going to do, write my answers for me?"

He smiled. "Yes."

"How?"

"Easy." He beamed at me like sunrise on a cloudless day. "I slip into your tutor's head and find out the exam questions. Then I slip into your mind and tell you the answers. I imagine you can take it from there."

"You, possess me? Are you crazy?"

"Fine." He stood up in a rush and barged past me. "You don't want my help, you don't have to take it. I'd say *au revoir*, but I don't suppose we'll meet again. Not if you don't qualify."

"Wait." The word shot out of me before I could stop it, like farting in church. "All right," I said, "I'm desperate, but isn't there some other way? Apart from—?"

"Make your mind up," he said. "If you want to give it a go, fine. If you don't, also fine. But if we're not both out of this sucker's head in the next ten seconds, he's going to have an aneurysm and die. You'd have known that if you'd bothered going to lectures."

But I did know that, only I'd forgotten. "All right," I said, "it's a deal. But no obligations."

"You're a hard man to do a favour for, you know that?"

We left together, rubbing metaphorical shoulders as we scrambled for the way out (down the eustachian tube, turn left at the tympanic cavity and follow your nose) Outside he dissipated like smoke or a swarm of bees. The elderly drunk sat up and gawped at me. I bought him a drink. It was the least I could do.

Out in the open air, I thought about what I'd committed myself to, and it occurred to me that I'd managed to do an amazingly remarkable thing; I'd found a way to make my previous situation worse. I almost felt proud. Not many people could've done that. Quite an achievement.

The sensible thing would be to go to my tutor and confess. At least then I'd be able to warn him to be on his guard. It meant I'd be thrown out of the Studium before the exam rather than after it, but that would save my father a week's board and lodging, so no bad thing. I agonised about it for about four seconds, then set off for his lodgings.

He was there, reading *Gelimer on Moral Necessity*. He looked up at me and smiled. He never did that. He offered me a bowl of tea and a honeycake. What's got into him, I wondered. Then it struck me that I knew exactly what had got into him. Say what you like about the legions of the Prince of Darkness, they don't stop to let the grass grow under their metaphorical feet.

I'd already started the sentence. "I've done a terrible thing," I heard myself say.

My tutor nodded. "I know. It's no big deal. Don't worry about it."

I thanked him and left.

Say not the struggle naught availeth. True, I'd struck a bargain with the Evil One to obtain an unlawful advantage, but that didn't mean I was going to take advantage of that advantage. It would still be my hand moving the pen across the paper in that horrible circular room. So what if some hellspawn inside my head told me all the right answers? Nothing to stop me writing down the wrong ones. It wouldn't make it right, but at least I could mitigate my crime to a small (but significant) extent. On the day of the exam I turned up an hour early, with my pen, my inkhorn and my penknife, and hung around looking mournful until the invigilators opened the doors and shooed us inside. I sat down at my place on the bench next to a man I knew slightly and didn't like much, and rehearsed slowly and carefully the one Form I'd thoroughly revised the night before. It was *sicut in terra*, the Form for closing your mind to a hostile intruder. When he came, I'd be ready for him.

The chief invigilator cleared his throat and read out the questions. I copied them down automatically, realising that I knew all the answers.

Made no sense. I muttered *sicut in terra* under my breath anyway, just in case, but it didn't matter. If he came, I could simply tell him to get lost, because I didn't need him. All the correct answers had been inside my head all along; I must have absorbed them subconsciously while daydreaming or hung over in lectures, and the fact that I hadn't revised them didn't matter a damn. The information had been in my memory all along and I hadn't realised it. Good old brain, I said to myself, I never doubted you for a minute.

I wrote quickly and finished with time to spare, which clearly annoyed my neighbour, who was still scribbling frantically when the bell went. I smiled at him when we got up to leave. I knew I'd scored at least ninety-two per cent; probably a record. Clever old me.

Traditionally, students celebrate the end of their Finals by drinking until they're reduced to the level of brute beasts, but I wasn't in the mood. Instead, I went and flopped down by the fountain in the Sanctuary Yard. I'd bought a loaf of stale bread from one of the vendors in Coalgate, and I sat there picking bits off it to feed the carp in the fountain pool. It was a warm afternoon, birds were singing in the lime trees, and the splash of falling water was soft and soothing, like rain on the roof at night. I guess I must have fallen asleep—

He was sitting next to me, looking just like the miserable bastard beside me on the bench during the exam. "There now," he said. "That wasn't so bad."

"No, it wasn't," I said. "And I did it without you."

He laughed. "Don't kid a kidder," he said. "Just say thank you and be grateful."

"But you weren't in there. I kept you out. I used *sicut.*"

He sighed. "If you'd been paying attention in lectures," he said, "you'd have known that *sicut* doesn't work against an intruder who's already in place. Though I resent the term intruder. As I recall, I was invited."

He'd been inside my head all the time. Since when? Since I went to see my tutor? I had no idea.

My stomach suddenly heaved.

"Tsk," he said. "I gather it's standard operating procedure to throw up in a fountain after Finals, but I think you're supposed to drink something first. You'd better get going before the proctors arrive."

He had a point. I got to my feet and wobbled. My head felt like it was full of something. I realised I was awake, and there was vomit all over the fountain steps.

"Sorry about question six," he said, inside my mind. "Truth is, I don't know that one. I never did get around to reading Prudentius."

"Get out," I yelled aloud, but he'd already gone.

I passed. I got ninety-five per cent, a record which stands to this day. My tutor was delighted. Of course, he said, I never doubted you'd come through with flying colours. I always knew you had it in you.

I waited and waited for payback time. You can't let a demon do you a favour and expect to get away with it. It's not possible. It makes no sense. Except—

I'm still waiting.

"So that's what they are," she said. "Well, then. I really don't see that there's a problem."

"Think about it," I said. "For some reason I can't begin to speculate about, there are no demons in Idalia. You want to take one there. Can't you see what's wrong with that?"

"No."

I took a deep breath and didn't shout. "There are no demons in Idalia. Three possible reasons for that. No, make that four. One, they don't know about you. Two, they can't exist in your climate. Three, there used to be a long time ago but you somehow managed to get rid of them. Four—" I'd forgotten what the fourth reason was. "Either there *can't* be demons in your country, in which case you're wasting your time, or else there *can*, in which case you risk infesting yourselves with them, which is potentially catastrophic. You have absolutely no idea what they're capable of. The only reason human life can survive here in the west is because we, the Studium, keep the little horrors strictly under control. We can do that because we've got five thousand years' worth of experience and knowledge, desperately hard won. You're planning to import them and set them loose to fight your war, and you don't know the first thing about them. It's like deciding to keep bubonic plague as a pet."

"I'm sure we can handle them," she said blithely. "It can't be hard, or you couldn't do it."

"What exactly happened? When you killed the prior."

"I wish you wouldn't keep banging on and on about that."

"What happened?"

A thoughtful look settled on her lovely face. "I'm not sure, exactly," she said. "After I got rid of you at that inn place, I wandered about in the market district for a bit, wondering how I was going to find out about this weapon you're supposed to have that we need but don't know about. And the next thing I knew, I was climbing out of a window and there was blood all over my hands. That's all I remember. I've only got your word for it that I killed anybody."

"My word and the City Watch."

"Maybe you told them I did it, I don't know. You haven't really given me any reason to trust you."

I tried to make sense of what she'd told me, but it was like trying to put a frightened cow in your pocket. "That's all you remember."

"I just told you that. I wish you'd listen."

"So you were roaming around in a public place, *wanting* to attract a demon—"

"I suppose so, yes."

"And look what happened. The unprovoked murder of a high-ranking religious leader."

"So you tell me. I don't know that."

"Tell me something," I said. "Is there any conceivable way of making that sound like a desirable outcome? Maybe I'm being stupid today, but I can't think of one."

She shook her head. "Teething troubles," she said. "Like when Na invented thunder powder."

"Who's Na and what the hell is thunder powder?"

"You know." She frowned. "Maybe you don't. Thunder powder. What people use in [weird Idalian word] and [another weird Idalian word]. For blowing things up. No? Gosh. Anyway, it doesn't matter. The point is, the first time it was discovered, the man who discovered it was killed and half a city was reduced to rubble. But after a fairly short time we figured out where he'd gone wrong and how to do it right, and now we've got an incredibly useful and beneficial artefact that we put to all kinds of good uses, completely under our control." She gave me a warm, understanding smile. "You're afraid of these demons because you don't understand about them. Probably that's why you've convinced yourselves that they're some sort of dark spirits serving some nebulous Prince of Evil. It's because you're primitives. You don't understand scientific method. You live by superstition and fear, instead of enlightened logic. I'm prepared to bet these demon things aren't nasty little men who burrow into your head, they're how you perceive a perfectly ordinary natural phenomenon, like magnetism or lightning. I bet you people think lightning is the anger of the gods. It's not. It's an accidental discharge of cosmic energy, ignited by friction when it pierces the bulwark of the clouds. Nothing *supernatural* about it at all. But to unsophisticated primitives like you, it looks like magic. Probably the same with these demons. I don't suppose they're even alive. You've just convinced yourselves they are, that's all."

Something I've noticed about people. The smarter they are, the dumber they can sometimes be. There's something about great wisdom and learning that unlocks a person's vast latent capacity for doing really stupid things, when the opportunity presents itself. "It's not a thing, it's a—" I was about to say person. "It's alive and it thinks for itself. And it's smarter than you are. You may find that hard to believe, but it's true."

That earned me an indulgent smile. "How would you know?"

"I know about them," I said, "the way a beekeeper knows about bees. You do have bees in Idalia, don't you?"

"I see. You farm them. You draw off the evil."

You can see it in someone's eyes, the dreadful moment when you put an idea into their head that would never have got there if you'd kept your mouth shut. "No, I didn't mean that. Not bees. Wasps."

"You can't farm wasps, they don't make honey. But these creatures of yours—"

What had I done? "It was a really bad analogy," I said. "They're nothing like bees, but very like wasps. Make that hornets. The only thing you can do with them is smoke them out so they go away."

The smile warmed up and widened, God help me. "When the First Emperor was being besieged by his enemies and they tried to dig saps under the walls to make them collapse, the Emperor ordered his men to gather up all the hornets' nests in the city. They dug into the enemy saps and threw the hornets' nests in. A few days later, the enemy gave up and went away. That's how wasps saved the Empire." Her face was radiant, like the sun. "Everything can be useful and everything can be made to serve the glorious purpose of true virtue. You've just got to have a little imagination, that's all."

Someone, I forget who, once said that there are only two sorts of people in the world, friends and strangers. Love your friends, the hell with strangers. I'm all for that, as a general rule. The acid test must always be; what harm did he ever do me, what good did he ever do me? Except—

I lunged at her with *velut fulmen*. It's a wonderful Form. It comes out of nowhere and glides through most types of shield as if they weren't there. Even if your shielding works, it hits you so hard you're left stunned and reeling, like a soldier in full armour hit with a sledgehammer. The only reason it's not more widely used is that it's difficult, but I can do it easy as sneezing. Because it's not in the usual repertoire nobody expects it. The only drawback is, it gives you a slight nosebleed, but so what?

It bounced off. It's not supposed to do that.

"Did you just hit me?" she said.

"No."

She shot me a poisonous look, and then the ground opened and swallowed me up.

I HATE IT when that happens.

I came round with blood trickling into my mouth, from the nosebleed. It was dark, and I was lying at an awkward angle, which hurt my back. High above me I saw a long, thin slit of light; the open sky above the ravine she'd opened under my feet. The bitch, I thought. Now, how do I get out of this?

I tried to stand up, but the space I was confined in was too narrow. The walls of the ravine were sheer and smooth, like glass. I scrabbled at them with my hands and my fingertips squeaked. It suddenly occurred to me that unless someone happened to come along with a very large coil of rope over his shoulder and notice me down there, I was probably going to die. The violent access of terror that followed was like a very heavy weight resting on me, not quite heavy enough to crush my bones but not far short of it. I tried breathing, but my chest muscles weren't strong enough to lift the weight. I can't begin to tell you what it was like, the unexpected and very real possibility that in a few days, a sun would rise that I wouldn't be there to see; a world without me, carrying on perfectly normally on the surface, but from my perspective with one small but important element missing. So this is it, I thought. Shit.

That bloody woman. Had she really meant to kill me, or had she meant it as no more than a useful tactic for getting rid of an annoyance, assuming that I knew some Form or other for fishing myself out of very deep holes? Maybe they had just such a Form where she came from, one that they teach to twelve-year-olds as a simple way to ease them into the curriculum. Or maybe her temper had flared up, and she neither knew nor cared what the consequences would be. Wouldn't surprise me in the least. In a country where adepts were the rulers, what incentive would you have to care? Just like we have no real reason to mind where we're putting our great big feet when walking among ants.

And these people were under the impression that demons might come in handy. Oh boy.

Not that it mattered. They lived a very long way away, and they were much more likely to wipe each other out than come together in unity to embark on world conquest. The demons were welcome to them, though I wasn't entirely sure that they were welcome to the demons. Like the old joke about the palace falconers; why did they start feeding the hawks on lawyers instead of rats? Well, under certain circumstances you can grow attached to a rat.

Or a demon; at least when compared with some of the more extreme examples of my own species. Which raised the question—not exactly at the forefront of my priorities at that moment, but there was nothing else I could do while stuck in a hole except think, and I had time on my hands—of what constitutes us and them, and where my loyalties ought to lie. Now don't get me wrong;

I believe unshakably in us and them, the great polarity
that defines everything, what Basso the Fortunate calls
the doctrine of Sides. In a world divided between day
and night, land and sea, living and dead, human and animal, all the countless binary distinctions by which we
make sense out of chaos, it's inevitable. You're defined by
the side you're on, and there are always sides. Morals and
ethics come and go, fluid and mutable as the whims of
dressmakers and milliners. This year we wear our beards
long and we hate Blemmyans and homosexuals, next
year everybody's sporting moustaches with chinstraps
and universal tolerance and understanding, and the only
thing reliable and constant is that next year everything
will be different, and we'll all be ashamed and horrified
about how we used to look and we'll make a solemn vow;
platform heels, never again. But sides—your family, your
clan, your tribe against everybody else—that's forever.
And it's not something you think about, agonise over
or choose; you *know*, every time you look in a mirror. I
belong to this family, this clan, this tribe, this guild, this
nation, and everybody else is the enemy.

Except—

I know which side I'm on. I'm for light against darkness, heaven against hell, human against demon. I knew
it before I was old enough to think, and then I went to
the Studium, where they taught me what I already knew,
but with rational explanations for all my instincts. I'm
for Good against Evil, and I don't care who knows it. I'm
for Good, right or wrong.

In which case, I was for her, against my friend.

There's not a lot to be said in favour of being stuck in a crevasse in a derelict tannery, but it gives you time to think. I thought for a long time, and then I heard a voice calling my name.

I looked up. Impossibly high up above me was a face. Someone I didn't know, a stranger, but he knew me. "It's all right," he was yelling, "I'll get you out of there in two shakes. Stay calm. Don't go away."

The face vanished. Very few people know my name. Maybe, I thought, she's realised what she'd done and sent someone to get me out. I waited for what seemed like a very long time and the stranger came back, with a rope. He told me to tie it round myself under my armpits, which I did. Then he pulled me out.

By the time I reached the top he was exhausted with all that pulling. His hands, I noticed, were red raw and bleeding. "Thank you," I said.

"'S all right," he gasped. "No skin off my nose, obviously."

I looked at him. A big man in his early thirties, well-dressed, expensive shoes, fashionable hair done that morning at one of the good barbers' shops in Haymarket. Never seen him before in my life. Not used to hard manual labour. He was a wreck.

"It's you, isn't it?" I said.

He nodded. "You all right?"

"I'm fine," I said. "Thanks to you."

"I always seem to be getting you out of deep holes," he said. "Though this one you didn't dig for yourself, which makes a nice change."

"Who's he?"

"What? Oh, him. First warm body I could lay my hands on. He'll be all right, once the rope-burns heal up. You look like you could use a drink."

"Not just now," I said. "What happened?"

"I was about to ask you that."

"You first."

No big deal, my friend told me. He'd sensed that I was in trouble, so he grabbed the nearest human and came to find me. Perceiving that I was stuck down a hole, he got a rope. The human had pulled me out, and there we were.

"Why?" I asked him.

"Excuse me?"

"You saved my life. Why would you do something like that?"

He laughed. "It's my job," he said. "It' what I do. Evil. I possess people."

"Yes, but—"

He contorted the face of the complete stranger into a happy grin. "I swooped down on a defenceless human, penetrated his body, usurped his mind, forced him to do my will." He held up his hands. "See? Your actual blood and tissue damage. I earn extra points for that. I'll probably get a commendation."

"That's not why you did it."

He gave me that wise look. "Believe it or not," he said, "there can be more than one reason for doing something. I've just given you a valid reason. Now, then. Your turn. What were you doing down that hole?"

I told him. He frowned. "I thought she was on your side."

"Apparently not. What did she do to you?"

He looked sad. "I can't tell you. You know that. If I try—"

I nodded. Then I took a deep breath and jumped into his head.

NOT HIS HEAD, of course; the head of his host, the well-dressed man who'd unwittingly and unwillingly saved my life.

"What do you think you're playing at?" my friend yelled at me. "Seriously, you're not going to chuck me out, are you? After everything I've—"

"Calm down," I said. "I'm going to get to the bottom of this if it's the last thing I do. I told you what that crazy bitch told me. She wants to take a demon back to Idalia, to use as a weapon. Do you honestly think that's a good idea?"

"It's not up to me."

A curious choice of words. "You can't tell me what's going on, can you? Your superiors won't let you."

"That's right."

"Not willingly, anyway."

He gave me a shocked look. "Now just a minute—"

"You can't," I said, "volunteer information. But you're not responsible for what you say under coercion. After all, I'm a hell of a lot stronger than you."

"Yes, but—"

"I could beat it out of you," I said, "and your bosses couldn't have you for it. No board of enquiry could possibly convict you, not if you showed them the bruises."

He backed away. "That would imply there were bruises to show."

"We humans have a saying. Omelettes and eggs."

"For crying out loud," he said, as I moved toward him. "You're supposed to be my friend."

While I'm beating the metaphorical crap out of my friend, let's pause for a moment and consider the concept of greater love.

Greater love, says the user's guide, hath no man than this, that he lay down his life for his friend. I wouldn't argue with that, but it's not the whole story. Greater-but-one love, one notch down from the absolute pinnacle, is kicking your friend's head in and jumping on his ribs *for his own good*. There's that old lie teachers tell you when they give you twelve strokes of the lash for not having learned your irregular verbs; this is going to hurt me more than it hurts you. Like hell. In this case, though, I suggest it wasn't all that far from the truth. But if the only way I could help him was by smashing his bones into splinters, so be it. I hated doing it. I think I'll leave it at that, if you don't mind.

"Right," I said. "Let's hear it."

He was a mess. As I think I may have mentioned already, I'm good at that sort of thing. I can break the will of a demon if I absolutely have to. He looked at me and called me something or other.

"Please?" I said.

He let out a very long sigh. "I'm not sure what happened, really," he said. "I was snuggling down deep inside that corn-chandler when I got a memo from Area Command; go to the *Flawless Diamonds* and stand by. No explanation, no context, nothing. So I went there, and next thing I knew, it was like being sucked into a quicksand or a whirlpool. This lunatic woman—"

"I know," I said. "I met her, remember?"

He nodded. "I couldn't actually tell you who did what to who. It was the weirdest feeling. I'm used to being cast out, it's just another day at the office as far as I'm concerned, but being cast *in*—"

"Then what?"

He looked grave. "All hell broke loose. Let me tell you something, I've been around. I underachieve and keep my head down doing the absolute bare minimum of work because in my time I've done stuff and seen stuff— Let's just say, after a while, even someone like me feels the attraction of the quiet life. I mean, it was all fine by me, I'd never dream of questioning the decisions of Area Command, but even so—" He stopped and drew a deep breath. "There are some things you find yourself having to do in the line of duty that stay with you, is all I'm saying. I don't feel guilty or anything like that, but maybe that's why I've been so nice and helpful to you over the years. Maybe I felt— Anyway, the hell with all that. The point I'm trying to make—"

"Consider it made," I said. "Go on."

"Never seen anything like it in all my years in the service," he said. "The worst part about it is, I don't even know if it was her egging me on, or me controlling her." He stopped, thinking. "Ever do any alchemy?"

"A bit."

"Well, then. Suppose you mix aqua ferox with sal draconis. Ever try that?"

"Once. Never again."

"Quite. Now, you tell me. Is it the aqua ferox's fault, or the sal draconis'?"

"Neither," I said. "It's just that when you mix the two, bad stuff happens."

"I think that's how it was with that wretched woman and me," he said. "I don't think either of us was in control. All I can remember clearly is this voice in my head saying, let's do the worst possible thing we can. I know, let's murder a prior. But it wasn't her saying it, I'm sure of it. And I'm damn sure it wasn't Area Command."

I wasn't sure I liked the sound of that. "You two had a bad reaction?"

He nodded. "I think that's why there's none of us in Idalia," he said.

"The implications—"

"Tell me about it," he said grimly. "Only I wouldn't dwell on it, if I were you. I'm much smarter than you are, so maybe you won't ever realise the full significance. Lucky you."

"It's not just Good and Evil," I said. "There's another—"

"Like I said," he said firmly, "don't think about it. Tell yourself, this is just some shit that happens if you're not careful. All right?"

I looked at him. I know him too well. "There's more," I said. "They wouldn't let you talk to me about it. I had to beat it out of you. Therefore—"

He scowled at me. "Area Command doesn't want anyone knowing about this until they've had a chance to think it through and figure out how to deal with it. Meanwhile, it's very classified."

No, I thought, it's not just that. But I'd hurt him enough for one day. "Understood," I said. "I'm sorry."

"Yeah." He gave me a rueful look out of his one good eye. "Knowing that makes me feel a whole lot better. Get out."

"Excuse me?"

"You heard me. I'm responsible for this body, and you've been inside it far too long. So I'm casting you out. Begone, foul fiend, and all that stuff. Shoo."

I thanked him again and left him to put the body back where he'd found it. I had things to do.

Here's some excellent advice for you. If you're going to make a horrible mess, don't do it in Sabades Amar. It's too small and too far from anywhere. No backup. For example, we have no regular presence there, not even a part-time resident. The nearest professional colleague and link in the chain of command was the deacon at the priory at Olomenen, forty miles away over a distinctly awkward mountain pass. Even if I could get there and back in less than a week—I shuddered to think what that bloody woman might get up to in seven days—a mere deacon couldn't possibly be any help to me. All he'd be able to do would be to send a letter to the regional precentor at Thoas, who'd have no option but to refer the matter to the Dean of Humanities at Hiraut, who'd almost certainly need a ruling from GHQ before he could commit to anything. In practice, this far out of the loop, I was the Studium and the Studium was me. A cheerful thought as I wiped blood off my chin and hobbled on my twisted ankle up North Ropewalk towards the Haymarket.

Face facts, I told myself, nobody's going to help you or do it for you, you're going to have to kill her on your own. That, of course, is what being a high-level field grade is all about. You make the decisions, you carry them out, you take the blame afterwards. I suggest you think about that after Finals, when you're deciding which stream to apply for.

I had to find her first. Sabades is a small town compared with, say, Mondesir or Beal Regard, but it's hardly a village. I stood in the centre of Haymarket and sniffed until people started looking at me, but all I got was mundane urban stink, and I can savour that any day of the week back home. For all I knew, she'd already skipped town and was on her way somewhere else. In which case, said a wicked little voice in my head, she's no longer your problem. All you have to do now is catch the next coach to Olomenen and file a report with the deacon. That's all that's required of you, and it's the right and proper thing to do, according to established procedures. In fact, it's what you should do, what you *have* to do, and anything else would be exceeding your authority and probably a court-martial offence. It would be Wrong, and Wrong is next door to Evil—

Absolutely. And by the time I got to Olomenen, that ghastly woman might well have found a demon, conjured it into an oil bottle and caught the express to Beloisa, where a ship was waiting to take her back to Idalia. But (said the little voice) Idalia is a very long way away, and distance doesn't just lend enchantment, it purges guilt. All sorts of truly awful things happen in foreign parts, everybody knows that. They have earthquakes and tidal waves and plagues and famines and droughts and truly appalling wars, but all that is no concern of ours, because it takes place somewhere else among strangers, and can't possibly be our fault. If it wasn't like that, life would be intolerable. Every time some bunch of improvident idiots got themselves in trouble somewhere, we'd feel obliged to do something about it. You couldn't live like that, what would be the point? Why bother with all the gruelling labour of ploughing, planting, weeding, reaping, binding, thrashing and milling, when at any moment a messenger might arrive from South Blemmya and tell you there's famine in the Oulang and all your surplus grain is needed to feed the starving children? In effect you'd be a slave on your own land, breaking your back and getting nothing more out of it than your bare subsistence. Screw that. Am I my brother's keeper?

I considered the little voice. It wasn't a demon, it was me. Sometimes, it's hard to tell the difference.

Back to practicalities. Last time I saw her, she was still very much wanted by the civil authorities. I don't have much time for them as a rule, but they have their uses. You don't have to be a tenured professor of meta-physics to send a couple of steelnecks to keep an eye on the coach depot and the three livery stables. No way of knowing what an Idalian might be able to do by way of supernaturally assisted transport, but the fact that she'd come in on a coach suggested to me that if she wanted to get from A to B, she'd have to do it the same way as everybody else; boats, horses, feet. The same considerations, I felt reasonably confident, would have occurred to the deadheads at the City Watch. She wasn't going anywhere.

Therefore she was still in town; therefore she was still on my To Do list, therefore I was going to have to kill her. Bummer.

When all else fails, use your intelligence. Here we have a wanted fugitive from a distant land unimaginably different from the place she now finds herself in. She's alone with no resources or backup. True, she has very impressive supernatural abilities, but they're limited in scope (limited to what extent we unfortunately don't know). She also has a job to do, and all the evidence tends to suggest that she's conscientious about doing it. Furthermore, her attitude to date gives reason to believe that she's confident, overconfident, cocky; when rescued from prison she's not particularly grateful, she regards the locals with tolerant amusement, she thinks she's better than we are, most likely because she is. Therefore—

"How on earth did you manage to escape from that hole?"

I spun round. She was frowning at me, as though she'd only bought me the day before and already my seams were starting to split. "You," I said.

"I thought I smelt you," she said, "but I thought no, it can't be. Maybe I was wrong. Maybe you're not as pathetically stupid as you look."

On my To Do list, round about number three, was find a cutler's shop and buy a dagger. I hadn't got round to it yet, so I couldn't cut her throat where she stood. That's what you get for procrastinating. "For crying out loud," I said. "Why can't you just piss off and leave me alone?"

"I need you," she said briskly. "I need you to help me find that *thing.*"

I breathed out heavily through my nose. "Then you shouldn't have tried to kill me, should you?"

"You started it. You hit me."

"Of course I hit you. You wouldn't listen."

You're going about this the wrong way, said the little voice inside my head that wasn't a manifestation of the Evil One. If you really want to kill her, don't piss her off. Conciliate, lull, lure. Make her think you're on her side. It's so much easier to stab a friend than an enemy. They don't expect it. "I'm sorry," I said. "I was wrong. I shouldn't have hit you."

"Of course you shouldn't. For one thing, I'm a *girl.*"

Absolutely; in the same way that a man who's murdered his father and mother deserves our pity because he's an orphan. "Indeed you are," I said. "So, what can I do to help?"

That's more like it, she didn't need to say. "You know where to find it," she said. "The thing."

"No. Not offhand," I added quickly. "I can't conjure it up or anything like that. But I know its habits. We can look for it together."

I saw her relax. "That's better," she said. "Where do we start?"

Good question, given that my main objective at that point was not finding my friend. "A crowded public place," I said. "That's exactly where a demon would be likely to be."

"I'm not sure about that," she said. "The soldiers are looking for me. It might not be a good idea."

"What you need," I said, "is a disguise. Can't you magic yourself so you look different?"

She gave me that look. "No," she said, "don't be so stupid."

"I don't know, do I? If you can open holes in the ground, I'd have thought you could do a simple thing like change your appearance."

She sighed. "I don't know where all this hostility's coming from," she said. "After all, I'm doing you a favour. I'd have thought, if I take one of these things away with me, it'd be one less for you to have to deal with. You ought to be grateful, not making sarcastic remarks all the time."

"We got off on the wrong foot," I said. "My fault, I'm sorry. And yes, you're right, it wouldn't be sensible for you to go strolling about in a public place. On the other hand, that's where he's likely to be. You see the difficulty."

"It doesn't have to be a magic disguise," she said. "A big coat and a floppy hat would probably do the trick."

"You found him the last time."

As I spoke the words, it occurred to me that maybe I'd have done better to keep my face shut. How, after all, would I know that? But she didn't seem to have taken the point. "Not really," she said. "I think we sort of found each other. But now I think it's scared of me or something. Though that's not possible, is it? I mean, not if it's just magnetism or a strong ectoplasmic field or something like that. It can't *think* or anything."

You don't need a knife, said the little voice, you could strangle her with your bare hands. Shows how little the voice really knew about me. Besides, I was going off the idea. Killing people is fine in theory or at a safe distance (see above) but up close and personal, it's such a profoundly intimate act. Besides, she was probably stronger than me, or trained in arcane martial arts. I could just about have stuck a knife in her back when she wasn't looking; a nice sharp, thin one that'd go in with practically no effort. Anything more than that was out of my league.

"Maybe this isn't such a good idea," I said. "If you can't control it, I mean. What's the use of a weapon you can't control?"

"Only because we haven't had a chance to study it properly. You're too impatient, is your trouble. If you can't make it work first time, you just give up."

I wasn't paying attention. I'd just caught sight of someone I knew.

LET ME TAKE you back to my Finals. You may recall the man sitting next to me, the one I knew and didn't like much. He went on to become the senior lecturer in metaphysical theory at Listracon, a job I'd have given my right arm for. Not only that; he also managed to finagle a seat on the security committee and membership of the House of Deacons. In theory, he was four links above me in the chain of command. Fortunately, he was idle as well as objectionable and rarely went more than twenty miles from Listracon, except when he attended meetings at the Studium, so the risk of my running across him was acceptably slight. The chances of him turning up in Sabades Amar—

"There's a man over there looking at us," she said.

"I know. Pretend you haven't noticed."

"The hell with that. I'm going to splat him."

Music to my ears, under anything like normal circumstances. "No, don't do that."

"It's all right," she said cheerfully. "I can make it look like a seizure or an epileptic fit. Even a doctor can't tell the difference. And while everyone's fussing round him, we can quietly walk away."

Yes, we could do that, and it wouldn't be my fault. The little voice in my head had quite a bit to say on the subject. I'd like to be able to say that I wasn't tempted, not even for a split second. As it was, I was still dithering when he crossed the street and headed straight at us.

"Do you know him?" she said.

"Yes."

"Then why didn't you say so, you idiot?"

He looked me in the eye. "Is this her?" he said.

"What?"

"The Idalian. Is this her?"

"I'm Idalian," she said. "Are you Archdeacon Carinus?"

I opened my mouth to yell, but he cut in before I could get started. "You clown," he said.

TEN MINUTES LATER, in an empty charcoal shed behind the wheelhouse of an abandoned bonemeal mill, he really let go. I was, he told me, the worst, most stupid officer it had ever been his misfortune to serve with, and as soon as he got back to his office he was going to lodge a formal complaint with the General Synod demanding that I be demoted to Grade Six and permanently assigned to the lowest grade of administrative duty. Thanks to my stupidity, recklessness and arrogant presumption, an operation which had taken twelve years to plan and cost an incalculable amount of money, resources and political capital had been put in jeopardy; not only that, but the entire future of the Order itself now hung in the balance, thanks to my bull-headed ham-fisted interference. I had endangered innocent civilians, risked open conflict with the civil authorities—

"Hold on," I said. "What did I do?"

He glared at me, and his hands were balled into fists. "I can't tell you that," he said, "because it's classified. But believe me, you did it all right. And I'll see to it that you never work in the field again. That's a promise."

I looked past him at her. She shrugged. "Don't ask me," she said, "I'm not from around here."

"You stay out of it," he snapped. "Please," he added. "This is a strictly internal matter."

"Suit yourself," she said. "But I think you ought to tell him what he's done. That's only fair."

"I told you, stay out of it." He turned back to me and opened his mouth, but no words came out. He went bright red in the face and started clawing at his neck. Behind him, she smiled sweetly at me. "If there's one thing I can't be doing with," she said, "it's bad manners."

I looked at him. He looked at me. I saw that moment when he realised that I was perfectly capable of letting her kill him. Then I said, "It's very kind of you, but I think you should let him go now. He's a poisonous little turd, but over here, being a poisonous little turd doesn't carry the death penalty. Probably just as well, when you think about it."

He fell forward, gasping. I took a step back and let him slump to his knees. "About those charges," I said.

"All right," he muttered between deep, rasping draughts of breath. "Just keep her off me, will you?"

"After you've apologised to her for being rude. She's a guest in our country, after all."

He gurgled something with *sorry* in it. She nodded. "That'll do," she said. "Sincerity would've been nice, but I'm not fussy."

"And," I went on, "after you've explained to me exactly what's going on."

That made her frown, but he couldn't see her face. "Classified," he mumbled. I shook my head.

"Failure to explain," I said, "could be construed as extreme rudeness. I promise," I added, choosing my words carefully, "not to breathe a word to a living soul. Please?"

She took a step forward and her shadow fell across him. "All *right*," he snapped. "It's like this."

Luck; what does that word mean to you? It's something I've thought about a lot over the years, mainly because of our family history. My father was minor provincial nobility. We had an estate in the southern Mesoge. It sounded impressive in terms of sheer acreage, but a lot of it was covered by a substantial lake and most of the rest was mountains; all we got out of it was a bit of wool and some very low-grade dried fish which we sent down the mountain to Spire Cross, where City merchants paid us rubbish prices because of the transport costs. But my family were nominally Knights of Equity, which meant taxes, tithes, scutage dues and all the rest of it. When my grandfather died, we owed the government a lot of money in succession taxes, which we didn't have.

Not long after my grandfather died my father was out on the mountain looking for lost sheep when it came on to rain. Have you ever been to the Mesoge in summer?

We get these storms. They don't last long, but while they last you get wetter than if you'd fallen in the sea. So my father dived into a cave in the mountainside where the sheep liked to take shelter, and waited for it to stop.

While he was there, he noticed something twinkling. He looked closely and found a cluster of amethyst, about the size of a child's fist. He prised it out carefully with the tip of his knife, took it home, cleaned it up and took it down the mountain to Spire, where a merchant told him it was pretty mediocre stuff and only worth slightly more than what we owed the government in taxes. Money changed hands, my father paid off the dues and that, as far as he was concerned, was that.

Then, about three years later, we had that silly war with the Vesani and my father was assessed for double scutage, plus maintenance and chancel tax, and of course we hadn't got the money. So he went back to the cave with a lantern and poked about, and came home with two knobs of amethyst about the size of walnuts, and that was our family's contribution towards the Great Patriotic War for the Future of Civilization, which incidentally we lost. After that he paid three or four more visits to the cave, each time we needed an unanticipated windfall, and each time he came home with roughly the right amount of amethyst to get us out of trouble. His last trip to the cave was about a week before he died, and he dug out enough of the purple stuff to cover his succession taxes and leave a bit over for a decent headstone and a donative of fifty trachy a head to all the tenants. He was in perfect health right up to the day he dropped dead, in the home meadow on the third day of haymaking. I was at the Studium, of course, just finishing my internship in field work, so I missed the funeral.

When I got back, I found my brother Fortunatus in a high state of excitement. From now on, he said, things would be different. He knew all about the cave, of course. He was a dutiful son and our father had forbidden him to go inside, so he hadn't, but it was his cave now, and it was time we restored this family to its rightful position in society. For years he'd secretly fumed at the way the City merchants had ripped our father off, telling him the amethyst was medium-grade when it was the true dark stone, worth twice what they'd paid him. And he had plans. We were going to dam the lake and build a sawmill to saw the lumber from the forests on the mountain. And there was copper up there, he'd read a book about it and seen the telltale signs in the exposed rocks on the fell; we were going to carve off the whole of the top of the mountain, break the ore up with drop-hammers powered by the water from the dam, smelt it with charcoal from the forest and ship premium grade copper ingots by the cartload—not to the City, where they'd only rip us off, but down the other side of the mountain, to Angyra or Sirupat, where the Scona merchants came. Of course we'd have to build a road, but that would be no bother; and in the fulness of time we could build our own ships, take the stuff direct to Scona ourselves and cut out the middleman. In twenty years we'd be richer than palm oil, and then those stuck-up arseholes in the City had better watch out, because—

I stopped him there and questioned his choice of pronouns. Not *we*. I was just about to get my first field assignment; my future lay in the Craft, and if I never saw the horrible Mesoge again as long as I lived, I wouldn't be crying myself to sleep over it. My brother was shocked. Half of all this belongs to you, he said. You have it, I told him, I don't want it. Well, he called me various names and we parted, and I haven't seen him since.

Anyway, my brother set off for the cave with two dozen men, tools and carts, and they chipped out every last flake of amethyst, and they searched all the other caves and found nothing but bat-shit. No matter; my brother sold the lot in Scona and got a very good price for it; close on two hundred thousand nomismata, which wasn't quite enough to finance his imaginative development plans, so he invested every last trachy in a sure thing he'd been put on to by an old school friend of his, namely the Essecuivo Discovery and Trading Company. The Company fitted out a fleet of thirty-seven ships, all of which sank to the bottom of the sea in a freak storm, and that was the end of that. The last I heard of my brother, he was living in three rooms in the east wing of our old house with some girl from the village, two shepherds and a black and white dog. By all accounts he's reasonably happy, so that's all right.

Moral; trust to luck and it won't let you down, but you've got to wait for it to come to you. Go out looking for it and you'll scare it away. Trust me, I know about these things. I've got into enough scrapes in my time, mostly through my own stupidity, and yet here I still am, breathing, walking, not in jail. That can only be luck. No other explanation covers the known facts.

So I've learned to recognise luck when it pops up, and by the same token I have a pretty shrewd idea of when it's about to go away. It's almost as if it leaves a note for me on the table. From now on, it says, you're on your own. If you get out of this, it'll be because of your own skills, intelligence and moral fibre. I have every confidence in you. See you around, maybe.

I have a fair appreciation of my own skills, intelligence and moral fibre. They're not bad, if I do say so myself. Nevertheless, living my life without dumb luck is like trying to make bread without flour. I have no confidence in me whatsoever.

"It's like this," he said.

About five years ago, the Abbot of the Studium received a letter. It was addressed to the chief magician, the West, and it was written on black silk in gold ink, which is probably why the abbot read it instead of throwing it on the correspondence-from-nutcases pile. It was from someone purporting to be the head of the profession in Idalia, and it constituted an offer to open diplomatic relations.

Up to that point, the abbot had been a leading proponent of the no-such-place-as-Idalia school, but he was a good enough philosopher to admit he was wrong in the face of hard evidence. For one thing, the letter was written in a language so impossibly old and abstruse that only he and about four other scholars in the known world knew it; but he and three of the other four reckoned it represented the original language of our remote ancestors, back when they lived a very long way east, before the hypothetical great migrations. He figured, if some of our ancestors had gone as far east as the rest of them came west, Idalia would be more or less where you'd expect them to have ended up, assuming Idalia existed. More to the point, the letter could scarcely be a forgery concocted by one of his many enemies, because he knew everybody who was capable of having written it; they had their faults, God knows, but faking something like this wasn't one of them. Therefore the letter was genuine. There really was such a place as Idalia. And they wanted to talk to him.

The letter continued with two lists. One list, very long, was what they were prepared to give him. The other, very short, was what they wanted in return. The long list included powers the abbot didn't think were possible; flying through the air, turning base metal into gold, walking on water, travelling instantaneously over vast distances, assuming the shapes of animals and birds, transfiguring inanimate objects, foretelling the future and raising the dead. All this was possible and could be learned, and the Idalians knew how to do it and were prepared to teach him—him personally, please note; not a general licence to promulgate all these wonderful goodies among the adept community, at least not yet. They would be his alone, for as long as he lived.

Oh, and if he fancied immortality, they could arrange for that too.

In return—

"But of course," my idiot schoolfellow said, "the abbot would only use the powers for good. He's a man of unimpeachable integrity. He could no more commit a selfish or wicked act than—"

"Fly in the air?" I said. "Quite. Tell me what they want in return. No, don't tell me, let me guess. They want a demon."

He nodded. "That's all," he said. "In return for materials that would revolutionise the Craft and advance the sum of human knowledge to an unimaginable extent. It's the most amazing opportunity, even you must be able to see that."

I nodded slowly. "The sum of one man's human knowledge."

He made an impatient oinking noise. "The head of our Order," he snapped. "The single most respected individual in our entire community. Obviously, with knowledge of this sort, it would be out of the question to allow it to be freely available. It needs to be restricted, kept safe. It makes perfect sense for it to be concentrated in the hands of one exceptionally trustworthy man."

Perfect sense. Oh boy. "Has it occurred to you," I said, "that the demon isn't yours to give away?"

He stared at me, then burst out laughing. "You haven't changed," he said. "You always were an idiot.

And now your stupidity is jeopardising the single most important operation the Order has undertaken in the last two thousand years."

"That's me all over," I said, "thick as a brick. What was the game plan, before I showed up and started screwing things up for everybody?"

"The arrangement was for me to meet this young woman here and provide her with a demon to take back to Idalia. Then the Idalian adepts will send the abbot the promised materials."

"Fine. Any particular demon?"

"None specified," said the idiot, maybe a trifle defensively.

"You just figured you'd stroll through the streets of this minor provincial town until you happened to find one."

He glowered at me. "If you must know," he said, "the point you raised just now had occurred to us. We contacted various resources we have on the other side."

I felt like I'd just been hit over the head with a brick. "You mean," I said, "Evil?"

"If you insist on putting it in that ridiculously melodramatic way, yes. Naturally, we have established channels through which we can communicate with the opposite Orientation, as and when the need arises. We felt that it would be, let's say a breach of protocol to take one of their assets without at least giving notice of our intention to do so."

"You asked their permission to take a demon."

I was irritating him. Oddly enough, I didn't mind. "To avoid friction and possible confrontation, yes. We felt that it would facilitate matters and avoid the risk of anything going wrong if we presented the other side with a broad outline—"

"And you asked them," I said, "to choose you a specimen they wouldn't mind dreadfully losing, and they chose this one."

He gave me his killer look. "Yes."

"Thank you," I said gravely.

"They said that this particular demon would be, to quote their exact words, no great loss." He laughed, bless him. "And therefore they undertook not to make difficulties or take any steps beyond routine diplomatic protests to get him back. He's an embarrassment to the service, so you'll be doing us a favour getting him off our books, is what they said. They really were most reasonable about the whole thing."

Saints and ministers of grace preserve us. I looked at her. "Is this true?"

She shrugged. "Presumably," she said. "I was sent here to get a demon, that's all I know. I didn't know we were paying for one, but why would they tell me? None of my beeswax."

My head was starting to spin. "All right," I said. "But why did you kill the prior?"

The idiot gave me a furious but puzzled look. "I was going to ask you that," he said.

"You what?"

"That wasn't supposed to happen," he said. "It was completely unexpected and out of the blue. And, since your interference is the only part of the mission so far that wasn't carefully planned and risk-assessed before-hand, it's only reasonable to assume that it's somehow your fault. For which," he added with feeling, "you will answer before the proper authorities in due course. You have my word on that."

"Me?" I said. "What did I do?"

"I don't know," he snarled. "But you must have done *something*. Otherwise it wouldn't have happened."

"It wasn't his fault," she said. "Leave him alone. He hasn't done anything."

Nice that she was concerned, but puzzling. "He's an idiot," said the idiot. "You have no idea what he's capable of. I've known him since we were kids. He's an imbecile."

"He doesn't like me," I translated. "But never mind about that. Tell me what I could possibly have done to screw things up. I don't understand."

"Let's think about this sensibly," she said. "What did you actually do? You met me, in that rather seedy inn."

I nodded. "I figured out you were Idalian."

"Then what did you do?"

Awkward moment. I'd sort of told her earlier that the demon who'd joined with her in killing the priest was my friend, but did she know I'd talked to him shortly before it happened? Heaven help me, I couldn't remember. "Nothing," I said. "Until I heard about you being wanted for killing the prior."

"I remember now," she said, with a friendly smile on her face. "You kept wanting to know what I'd done to your friend."

The idiot looked at her. "What friend?"

"The demon."

THE THIRD TIME I met him was years later. I'd qualified and finished a two-year posting in Epitedeia, mostly possession work but with some teaching thrown in. I'd done a good job in Epitedeia, and when I got back to the Studium I had high hopes of a relatively quick and easy scramble up the ladder. By this point I'd decided that what I really wanted to do was teaching and research, possibly with a view to breaking into the bossing about and ordering around sectors, which appealed to me on an intellectual level. I wrote that stupid book, and people seemed to think it was pretty hot stuff. I taught a few classes and got good results, and the rest of the time I helped out generally, running errands and doing bread-and-butter work that my superiors were too grand or too lazy to bother with.

So, when a simple possession in aristocratic high society came up, I was all over it like gravy. The victim was the fourteen year old daughter of a junior senator, one of the coming men in the Optimate Tendency and a significant donor to the Studium social welfare fund. The fund paid the travelling expenses of field operatives outside the home provinces, so the senator had favoured civilian status; under normal circumstances, his daughter would have merited the personal attention of the Dean or one of the Lectors. As luck would have it, however, they were all out of town, and the highest ranking officer present, the Chair of Alchemical Theory, hadn't done a possession for twenty years and didn't trust himself not to kill the victim. He sent for me. I felt like I'd put my finger up my nostril and hooked out a thousand nomismata's worth of amethysts.

The girl was small, scared and sullen, with vomit down the front of her white silk gown and deep gouges on her cheeks where her maids had barely managed to stop her clawing out her own eyes. She was huddled in a corner of a vast, unbelievably beautiful room, unable to stand up because she'd broken her leg jumping off the top of the wardrobe. When I came in she threw a pen-knife at me. It missed me by a whisker. I paused to apply *lorica* and put on a big smile. Lying next to the bed I saw the body of a middle-aged woman in a clean, neat cream smock, lying with her head at a disastrous angle. Nobody else seemed to have noticed her, so I guessed she was probably a servant.

"Now then," I said. "What seems to be the trouble?"

The girl screamed at me, a long and fluent string of abuse in Old Permian, which by an extraordinary coincidence I'd taken as a supplementary dead language in Linguistics. She told me several things about myself, all of them true. One of them was that I'd cheated on my Finals.

I considered the damage, and the dead servant. Surely not, I thought.

The senator and his wife were looking at me; why doesn't he *do* something? They could see I'd been shocked by their daughter's tirade, and assumed I was scared. Which I was, in a sense, but not the way they thought. Anyway, it was time to be dynamic and powerful, so I was.

I slipped into her head like an eel through a net. The place was a disaster area. My friend was slumped in a corner, just as the girl was, and he was in a worse state than she was. But the injuries, I noticed, were several days old.

"You look awful," I said.

"Thank you so much."

I remembered the dead woman and the nail-gashes and the broken leg. "I misjudged you," I said. "I didn't think you were like this."

He laughed. "Why? Because I helped you? Oh come *on*. I do my job."

"I can see that."

He sighed. "You're right, actually. This sort of thing just isn't my scene. But I've been under a bit of pressure lately, from the regional brass."

I peered at his injuries. Their blood is purple, incidentally, or that's how it appears to me. It was caked in crystals on his forehead and round his mouth, like gemstones. By a real stretch of the imagination, amethysts. "Let me guess," I said. "You had a rough time in your last assignment."

"You could say that," he said with a grin. "I was under orders, stay in there until they drag you out by the roots. Turns out I have unusually tough roots. That," he added, "isn't exactly an unalloyed blessing."

Standard operating procedure. The code of practice says that the demon can't kill or irreparably harm the host when ordered to leave the body. But it's entirely legal to cling on tight. The effect is the same, but the actual damage is done by the exorcist, not the demon, so that's all right. According to the eggheads at the faculty of Law, it's all to do with who's active and who's passive. There's a lot of case law on the subject, apparently, but it's been regarded as settled for the last three hundred years.

"They're saying at Division," he went on, "that I've gone soft, I don't fancy it any more, one traumatic encounter too many with your lot. Apparently I'm now officially classed as fragile, would you believe. They're talking about taking me out of the field altogether and putting me on permanent desk duty." He shuddered slightly. "I don't want that."

"Is it so bad?"

He gave me a look I'll never forget. "In the field," he said, "I get to have a body. Not one of my own, naturally, but at least I'm *me*. Like one of those crabs that live in other creatures' shells. On desk duty, you're just— You start to drift apart," he said, and it was my turn to shudder. "After a bit, all that's left of you is what it takes to do the job. You don't need memories to correlate duty rosters, or a personality, or a soul—"

I tried to think about the dead woman outside. Somehow she didn't seem relevant.

"Anyhow," he said, "it was made pretty clear to me that I was on my final warning. Do a good job, they said, and everything's fine. Otherwise—" He closed his eyes for a moment. "I did a good job," he said. "They wanted the host damaged, I saw to it. He's going to spend the rest of his life in a chair in a dark room, just sitting."

"I'm sorry," I heard myself say. I think I meant it. I was young.

"We can't be hurt, of course," he said. "Which is to say, we're immortal, being composed of pure spirit, and any damage we sustain puts itself right in a day or so. But we can feel pain. We can remember it. I've been doing this so long, I can scarcely remember anything else. Maybe they're right about me, I don't know. If they stuck me in Clerical and threw away the key, most of what I wouldn't remember would be suffering." He lifted his head and laughed. "I'm sorry," he said, "you don't want to hear all this. Self-pity from the Common Enemy of Man, for crying out loud."

"It's all right," I said.

"Sure." He made an effort and sat up. "Look, I know I've got no right to ask this, but would you do me a favour?"

I felt a chill go down my spine. "Depends," I said.

"The senator," he said, "is on their shit list. The idea is, I put up such a fight coming out that the girl ends up a vegetable. This shocks the senator into a decline, and so he doesn't go on to unite the factions, drive through much-needed reforms of agrarian policy and improve the lives of countless generations yet unborn. They told me to wait till all the competent practitioners were out of town, so I'd get an inexperienced newbie who wouldn't be able to get me out clean. Someone," he added with a grin, "like you."

"Figures," I said.

"Which is where," he said, "they've made their mistake. I know you. The fact is, I taught you everything you know. Well, I gave you all the answers in your exam, which isn't quite the same thing, but close enough for dance music. I don't think I can stand another out-by-the-roots job. Can you get me out of here nice and clean? Please?"

I thought hard. "Can you make it easy for me?"

"No. They'd know if I did, and that'd be me up on a charge. We have a three-strikes rule. I'm on two. Have been for six thousand years, as it happens. Something like that hanging over you—" He shook his head. "I've got to fight you all the way. But I know you, you're good, quite possibly the best I've ever seen, one day. If I really try my best but I'm beaten by a superior opponent, that's fine, they're happy with that. I think you can do it, if you try."

I thought some more. There's a technique—a sort of flick of the metaphorical wrist—but it's dangerous. If it works, out the demon comes with no harm done to it or the host. If it doesn't, the outcome for the host is catastrophic, and you look like you ruined a human life just because you wanted to show off. I'd never done it before, but I knew how it was done. And it would be such a feather in my cap—

"You made her kill someone," I said.

He nodded. "Her nurse," he said. "She's fond of her parents, but the nurse is the only one she really loves. I made her throttle her until her eyes popped. The theory is, we get hardened to it over time, like you people killing chickens. That's the theory, anyway."

I tried to look at him but it wasn't easy. "If I manage to get you out clean, won't your people be upset? It'll mean their plan will fail."

He gave me a startled look, then roared with laughter. "Of course it will," he said. "Our plans always fail."

"Do they?"

"Oh for pity's sake." For a moment, I could've sworn he was angry with me. "Yes, always," he said. "We think of something clever, but you stop us, so we go back and reshape it into part of a longer game. That's what we do, we play the really long game, and every defeat you inflict on us in the short term becomes a building block in the really long game, the one that's mapped out so far in advance that none of you can see where it's going. That's just how it is," he added, seeing my reaction. "It's how we've been forced to grow. If you can't be a tree, be a vine. But that's all grand strategy, nothing to do with you and me. By the time your mistakes come to light, you'll have been dead for a thousand years. They won't be able to blame you because they'll have forgotten you ever existed."

I felt as though he'd pulled off a mask, and his own face underneath was indistinguishable from it. "Is that right?"

That amused him. "I'll still be there, of course, to get the credit. Only there won't be any, because some clown like you will have screwed everything up for us, at the very last minute. So we'll go back to the drawing board, and we'll reroute the plan so it comes out in another thousand years, same vine, different tendrils. And so it goes on, for ever and ever, world without end. Just be glad you're a mortal. You don't know how lucky you are."

While he'd been talking I'd seen what I was looking for; the fulcrum, though that's a completely misleading way of describing it, the tipping-point, also misleading, the spot to aim at. I dug into him just as he was telling me how lucky I was, and he screamed, and I was alone inside the senator's daughter's head, just as the knowledge of what she'd done came flooding in. I got out of there fast. There's enough unhappiness in the world without wallowing in other people's misery.

THE LONG GAME. If at nine-million-two-hundred-and-forty-six-thousand-six-hundred-and-eighty-fifth you don't succeed, try, try again. In the meanwhile, my friend.

"Your what?" the idiot roared.

"My friend," I said. "Actually, that's misleading. More of a contact. I use him occasionally to channel misinformation to the bad guys. It's a long-standing arrangement. They know all about it back home."

That was a lie, of course, but he had no way of checking. "You have a—a *relationship* with this—"

"Yes."

I almost felt sorry for him. Almost. He swelled up like he was going to explode, then turned away, unable to bear the sight of me a moment longer. "Let me get this straight in my mind," he said. "We set up this incredibly important exchange." He turned and glared at her. "You come here to get the demon. You just happen to bump into *him*—"

She nodded. "At the inn. I thought he might be you, but I realised he wasn't so I got rid of him."

"And *he* just happens to know this particular demon." He sucked in a very deep breath. "And then you just happen to find the demon for yourself, before I can catch it and hand it over."

"Oh," she said. "Was I supposed to wait?"

"Yes, it was all arranged, it was in the *briefing*." He was furious with her. Well, quite. People who don't read the briefing, for crying out loud. "But instead of waiting you went ahead and took the demon—"

"Actually he took me. At least I think he did. I can't actually remember."

"And a senior cleric gets murdered." He couldn't bear the sight of her, either. He was running out of directions to look in. "And he'd been talking to the demon shortly before it found you." He was close to tears. "I don't know," he said. "This whole operation is going to hell in a handcart. Someone's going to have to explain to the abbot what's gone wrong, and I really don't see why it should have to be me."

At which point something happened in my mind. It was as though I was in a dark cave, and a stray shaft of light happened to fall on a cluster of purple gemstones. It was so sudden and unexpected—like finding I knew the answers to a set of exam questions—that for a moment I looked around to see who else was in there. In vain. Nobody here but us humans.

I looked at her. She pulled a sympathetic face, then hit the idiot with something remarkably like *instar fulminis*. Every muscle in his body went taut, just for a split second, and then he dropped to the floor like a discarded shirt and lay there in a heap.

I knelt over him. He was still breathing. "I know," I said. "You're not allowed to kill people. Except—"

She shook her head sadly. "No exceptions."

"Pity," I said, though I guess I was relieved. Being complicit in an actual murder is above my pay grade. "All right," I said to her, "you can come out now."

"In a minute."

I wasn't prepared to argue. "When he wakes up, he's going to remember. And then we'll both be in the shit."

She thought about it. "I could go in," she said, "and you could drag me out again, but I might not come quietly, and there could be an element of collateral damage or friendly fire or whatever. It'd mean some poor sod will have to spend the next forty years feeding him with a spoon, but it wouldn't be you."

Temptation almost beyond endurance. "Get thee behind me," I said. "No, it's a sweet offer, but I don't think so."

She grinned. "He won't be in a position to make trouble. There are going to be big changes at the Studium shortly, you'll see."

I thought; let's not go there. "The body," I said. "Is she really Idalian?"

She rolled her eyes. "I thought you knew. There's no such place as Idalia. It's a myth."

"Oh. But I thought—"

"Gullibility in matters geographical," she said sternly, "clearly runs in your family. I seem to remember your brother lost all that money sending a fleet of ships to Essecuivo, another mythical destination. Do yourself a favour. Buy a map."

"All that money," I repeated. "While we're on the subject—"

"Oh come on," said my friend. "That's not fair."

"You put it there," I said. "In the cave."

My friend hesitated, then nodded. "Your father understood," he said. "Intuitively, I guess, I sure as hell didn't tell him. But I did lead him there, before you ask. See? I've been looking after you since before you were born."

"Why?"

He rolled his eyes. "The long game," he said. "The everlasting game. The game that we always lose, except—"

"Except nothing's really decided till it's over," I said, "and it can't ever be over, because it lasts for ever. Your actual paradox," I pointed out.

"So you were paying attention in Logic. If I'd known, I wouldn't have bothered taking notes for you."

"Because the game is never over, it can never be lost."

He grinned. "In theory," he said. "However, don't bet money on us to win. You can't afford it."

"Tell me," I said, "about the long game."

THE MAIN OBJECT of the exercise, he told me, was to kill the prior of Sabades. At the time of his death, my pal tod me, he was nothing special. But, in about eighteen months' time, he was due to experience a beatific vision which would transform his life. He would preach a new, compelling gospel, and thousands of converts, lay and adept, would flock to him. Result; both the church and the Order would be splintered into violently opposed factions, leading to two centuries of heresy, schism and ultimately war—

"Hang on," I said. "You wanted to *prevent* that?"

Do let me finish, he said. What's two centuries? Nothing. After two hundred years, a new orthodoxy would emerge and unite the known world into something not all that far removed from the Kingdom of Heaven on Earth. That was what Divisional Command was so eager to forestall. They'd been able to sell it to the Oversight Committee because Oversight isn't really interested in anything more than seventy years ahead. But the long game—

"I see," I lied. "Just shows how wrong I can be. I thought all of this was about discrediting the abbot of the Studium."

He smiled, snapped his fingers and pointed at me. "Give the man a big jar of olives," he said. "That was the second objective. You probably noticed that all the goodies we tempted the abbot with are strictly demonic powers."

"Flying, alchemy, transfiguration, speaking in tongues, necromancy. A bit obvious."

"Not to your precious abbot. And not to you, I suspect, until the penny finally teetered on the brink and dropped. We made up Idalia so he'd be tempted. And he was. Now your friend here will go home and tell all the abbot's enemies about how stupid and gullible he's been, and my guess is, he won't be abbot for very much longer. Which suits Oversight just fine, incidentally."

"Are you sure about that?" I said. "He may be an idiot, but he's done a fine job."

"He's got to go," my friend said, "in order to make way for someone better." He smiled warmly at me. "I shouldn't be telling you this, but what the heck. After he's gone, your stupid friend here gets the job—"

"Oh for crying out loud."

"Precisely. He gets the job. He's an absolute disaster, and after two years he's impeached. In his place, his peers elect a man who'll go on to become the greatest, wisest, most far-sighted and influential abbot in the Order's history. He'll be known as either the Wise or the Great, Division hasn't quite made its mind up about that yet. He'll rule the Order for fifty years, and generations yet unborn will look back on that time as a golden age." He giggled. "That," he said, "will be you."

I opened my mouth but I couldn't make a noise of any kind.

"With me, of course, to guide you. But that's fine, we're old friends, and would I steer you wrong? Of course," he went on, "after you've gone—a long time after—certain elements of your legacy will turn out to be the seeds of the Order's eventual decline and fall, so when the whole lot comes crashing down it'll actually be your fault. Well, our fault. But that won't happen for six hundred years, so I really wouldn't stress yourself out about it. The long game, you see. Oversight is thrilled at the prospect of you becoming abbot, by the way. They couldn't give a flying fuck what happens in six hundred years time." He smiled. "We never win," he said, "but we never lose either. Your lot never loses, but it never actually wins. I think there's a term in geometry that describes it."

I looked at him, or at the body he was inside. "You set me up," I said.

"Absolutely. I'm your friend. I set you up for life. Which means that every time you needed one, all you had to do was reach out and grab a fistful of amethyst. Thanks to me, you're going to get what you always wanted, and better still, it all comes free. No obligations. You'll be the greatest and best abbot ever, and they'll paint icons of you for a thousand years."

"Get thee behind me, you bastard."

"I've been behind you all the way," he said. "Behind every great man, there's a loyal and devoted demon. It's not a lie. It's not an illusion of kindness, or goodness, or friendship. I really and truly have been kind to you. You really and truly will be a wonderful abbot. I really and truly am your friend."

"Except—"

"Exceptions," he said, "prove the rule. Oh, in case you're worried, this host won't get in any trouble. She's the mistress of the Mezentine ambassador, so she's got full diplomatic immunity. You see? We think of everything. We're absolutely committed to the principle that the innocent shall not be made to suffer."

I thought about the dead nurse. But then, what do I know? Probably she'd done something bad, at some stage. My hands, by contrast, were spotlessly clean. "Did you have to make a monkey of me like that? You lied to me."

"You shouldn't have been here. That was just bad luck. Well, good luck, really, it'll make it easier for you to impeach your dumb friend, when the time comes. Some amethysts are just *there*. Be grateful and move on."

"Fine," I said, "except you lied to me."

"Yes, all right, I lied. I couldn't tell you what I was doing and you wouldn't go away. So I played a little game. It was fun. Then this idiot interfered, and I had to wind it up. So what?"

I looked at him. "You won't get away with it," I said.

He pulled a sad face. "We never do," he said. "But by the time it all goes pear-shaped, it'll have transformed and transfigured into something else. We keep going. We have hope. It's all we've got left."

"You're amazing," I said. "I really thought you were my friend."

"Was, am now and ever shall be, game without end, amen. I hope this won't spoil things between us," he said cheerfully. "Not a matter of cosmic significance if it does, I guess, but it makes life a bit more bearable if you get on well with the people you work with. I never meant to hurt you, you know."

To win us to our harm, the instruments of darkness tell us truth. Quite. And when all is said and done, he's my friend.

Except—